The Lost Tide Warriors

Also by Catherine Doyle

The Storm Keeper's Island

Catherine Doyle

Author of *The Storm Keeper's Island*

BLOOMSBURY
CHILDREN'S BOOKS
NEW YORK LONDON OXFORD NEW DELHI SYDNEY

For Jess

BLOOMSBURY CHILDREN'S BOOKS
Bloomsbury Publishing Inc., part of Bloomsbury Publishing Plc
1385 Broadway, New York, NY 10018

BLOOMSBURY, BLOOMSBURY CHILDREN'S BOOKS, and the Diana logo are trademarks of Bloomsbury Publishing Plc

First published in Great Britain in July 2019 by Bloomsbury Publishing Plc
Published in the United States of America in January 2020 by Bloomsbury Children's Books

Lettering by Patrick Knowles

Library of Congress Cataloging-in-Publication Data
Names: Doyle, Catherine.
Title: The lost tide warriors / by Catherine Doyle.
Description: New York : Bloomsbury, 2020.
Summary: Deserted by his magic, Fionn Boyle, Storm Keeper of Arranmore, sees the island beginning to wither and illness sweeping the land and must find a way to summon Dagda's army of merrows.
Identifiers: LCCN 2019020659 (print) | LCCN 2019022231 (e-book)
ISBN 978-1-5476-0272-8 (hardcover) · ISBN 978-1-5476-0279-7 (e-book)
Subjects: CYAC: Magic—Fiction. | Brothers and sisters—Fiction. | Grandfathers—Fiction. | Islands—Fiction. | Ireland.
Classification: LCC PZ7.1.D69 Los 2020 (print) | LCC PZ7.1.D69 (e-book) | DDC [Fic]—dc23
LC record available at https://lccn.loc.gov/2019020659
LC e-book record available at https://lccn.loc.gov/2019022231

Typeset by RefineCatch Limited, Bungay, Suffolk
Printed and bound in the U.S.A. by Berryville Graphics Inc., Berryville, Virginia
2 4 6 8 10 9 7 5 3 1

PROLOGUE

On a frosty winter morning, in the waters of a half-forgotten island, a merrow was swimming far from her home. Mist hung like a veil over the sea, clinging to her skin as she broke the surface: first a crown of coral and bone, then yellow eyes as wide as moons. A pale scar traced the curve of her jaw.

She stilled in the water.

There was a boy standing at the edge of the ocean. She could smell the sea salt in his blood.

She licked her lips.

Storm Keeper.

She remembered him.

The boy's eyes were shut, his breath puffing from him in a trail of clouds. He stuck his hand out and wriggled his fingers above the water. For a moment he stood completely frozen. Then his body hiccuped violently, as though something inside was trying to punch its way out. He snapped his eyes open, fear threading itself into his frown.

Magic.

The merrow drifted closer. The sun was climbing into an ivory sky, and soon the island would be full of people bustling along the strand, cars sputtering into life as shop windows lit up like lanterns. She shouldn't be here, by the shore . . . so near the voice that had been whispering to her from its depths. But she had come anyway—to gaze upon the boy who had stirred Morrigan from her endless sleep.

After all these years, he had finally come.

The boy groaned as a spark jolted from his fingertips. "Come on!" He kicked a clump of seaweed into the water. "Come on, you stupid thing!"

Trapped magic.

The merrow frowned. Time was wearing thin. She could sense darkness moving beneath the horizon, swelling like a sea of its own as it made its way across the world. Toward the island. Toward the boy. *This* boy.

Foolish Dagda. He will lead us all to ruin.

The boy picked up a rock and flung it into the air. The merrow followed its arc, her lips twisting as it landed with a *plop!* right beside her head.

One heartbeat—two heartbeats—and then he

spluttered into life. He charged toward her, the water sloshing around his ankles and then his knees and then his hips.

The merrow hesitated for the briefest moment before her senses reclaimed her. She dipped under the next wave, her tail disappearing in a sheen of burned silver.

Not now, she thought, as she speared her way back to the undersea. *Not yet.*

Her warriors were bound to another.

They would have to wait. For ruin, or the Tide Summoner.

Whichever came first.

Chapter One

THE TICKING CLOCK

Fionn Boyle lay sprawled on an old, threadbare couch and tried to scream himself awake. Somewhere in the back of his mind, he knew he was dreaming, but he couldn't open his eyes. He could only listen to the crooning voice that had made a home inside his head. It was hissing like a snake, burrowing deeper into his brain.

Tick-tock, the voice whispered. *Can you hear me, little Boyle?*

Fionn could see Morrigan in his mind's eye—her leering grin, too wide in her angular face.

Tick-tock, crumbling rock.

Three days, watch the clock.

She cackled, and a shadow came skittering toward him, its fingers reaching through the blackness of his mind. *Tick-tock, tick-tock, tick-tock . . .* The words grew frenzied, the pitch climbing until it was no longer a laugh but a scream. TICK-TOCK, TICK-TOCK, TICK-TOCK.

Get away from me! Fionn tried to yell, but the words bubbled in his throat.

His body was spinning like a tornado, his arms thrashing blindly as he tried to pull himself back to consciousness. The couch groaned underneath him, the rusted springs heaving from the effort. *Help me! She's going to claw my eyes out! Please—*

There was a loud *splat!*

Fionn jerked awake as something cold and slimy slid down his nose.

He sniffed. Was that . . . ?

"Ham," came a familiar voice. "It's crumbed."

Fionn peeled the slice from his face.

His grandfather peered over him, his blue eyes twinkling in the dawn light. "I'm afraid you were cycloning again." In one hand he held an open packet of sliced ham, and in the other a bright orange block of cheese. "I thought the ham might be more humane."

Fionn pushed the matted hair from his eyes. A familiar fist of heat was blazing in his chest, the knuckles of it rolling against his rib cage as if saying hello. The Storm Keeper's magic awake, just as he was.

Fionn sighed. "Couldn't you have called my name, like a normal person?"

"When have you ever known me to be normal?" said his grandfather, nibbling a corner off the block of cheese. "But besides that, I called your name eight times. I poked you three times and I shook you by the shoulders exactly once. The next logical step—"

"—was ham," said Fionn, dragging himself into a sitting position and laying the offending slice on the armrest.

"I'm afraid so, lad." His grandfather was watching him too closely, his brows raised above the tip of his horn-rimmed spectacles. "Was it the same again?"

"Tick-tock," said Fionn, with a grim nod. "The countdown continues."

Morrigan had been living in his head for many months, but two weeks ago his dreams had taken on a new sense of urgency. The voice, once disembodied and distant, now came with a countdown, grasping hands and clawing fingers, bloodless lips held too close to his ear. She was growing stronger, giddier.

"The countdown," said his grandfather now, "is somewhat concerning."

A breeze slipped underneath the window and

wreathed the couch. Fionn pulled the blanket close around him. Last month, winter had crept over the island, sewing itself inside the wind and howling through the cracks in the walls. There were ice crystals webbing the windowpanes, and sometimes in the night, when Fionn woke gasping, he could see his breath hovering like clouds in the darkness.

"Why don't you go and lie down in my room, lad?" suggested his grandfather. "The energy in there is very benevolent and handsome. And there's a nice storage heater that'll blow the socks off you."

"I'm awake now anyway," said Fionn, stretching his arms above his head and rolling his neck around until it clicked. Back in the summertime, he had surrendered his twin bed to his mother, insisting instead on taking up residence on Donal the shopkeeper's donated couch, which looked like it had been exhumed from a haunted house and smelled not unlike abiding despair. It creaked awfully in the night and made the little sitting room seem even smaller than it was, but Fionn knew it wouldn't matter where he slept—Morrigan would still find him.

He rolled onto his feet. "What time is it?"

"Time?" His grandfather was striding back into the kitchen. "You know very well I don't adhere to such arbitrary concepts."

Time.

Fionn drifted toward the candle flickering on the mantelpiece, the only lit flame in a room full of candles. The wax was growing shallower—less a candle now, and more a milky blue puddle. Of course, it wasn't *just* a candle to begin with. It was his grandfather's essence, all of his memories gathered up in one magical concoction, borne of blood and sea, burning all day and all night, racing toward its end.

Time. His grandfather had borrowed an awful lot of it.

The reminder made Fionn queasy. Lately, it felt like everything was out of his control. As the nights ticked by and Morrigan crept closer to his days, he couldn't help imagining himself as the controller of a runaway train. He felt the darkness seeping in around the edges of him, the sorceress's countdown ticking in time with his pulse. Something was going to happen. Soon.

She will wake when the boy returns, Ivan had told him once, all too gleefully. *She will rise when the Storm Keeper bleeds for her.*

Fionn had not bled for Morrigan since the day she had awoken, but he had not succeeded in putting her back to sleep either. His journey to the Sea Cave during the summer still haunted him. He had come so close to losing his sister, and then to drowning all alone in that endless darkness, with Morrigan laughing in his ear. The memory had grown hard and spiky, and often, when his thoughts wandered, he would find it digging into his ribs.

"Sandwich?" called his grandfather from inside the kitchen. "I'll share the ham but the last of the mustard is all mine, I'm afraid. It's whole-grain. And French. *Très* expensive."

"No, thanks." Fionn stared at the little flame on the mantelpiece. The magic inside him flared in recognition. He stuck his hand out above the glass trough, willing the flame to dance for him.

Come on . . . Come on . . .

Fionn was the Storm Keeper, the one the island had chosen to wield the elements in Dagda's name, for as long as his mind and body could bear it. The one to command earth, wind, fire, and water, at little more than a simple thought.

It was supposed to be easy. It was *supposed* to be seamless.

He ground his jaw, wriggling his fingers the way his grandfather had taught him. *Come on.*

The flame ignored him.

His face started to prickle.

Grow, he willed it. *Dance*.

His magic hiccuped in his chest, nearly toppling him over.

Fionn dropped his hand with a sigh.

The sitting room filtered back into focus, and he found his grandfather hovering beside him. "It will come, lad."

"It's been five *months*."

"Maybe it will take one more."

"I don't have one more!"

"For all we know, Morrigan is bluffing," said his grandfather unconvincingly. "Spooking you, for her own amusement. Trying to get in your head."

"She's already in my head, Grandad. I need to figure out my magic. *Now*."

His grandfather frowned at his sandwich. "It wasn't like this for me... It didn't require much concentration, really..." He moved his gaze to the candles filling the shelves around them—the Storm Keeper's magic—years of it, brewed and bottled. The same magic that now ran in Fionn's veins. "You could always try burning one..." He trailed off at Fionn's expression.

"The last time I used candle magic, I vomited and passed out," Fionn reminded him. "I'm already full of magic. I just have no idea how to get it out of—"

Fionn's attention snagged on the bookcase over his

grandfather's shoulder—the one he had pored over last night, restlessly counting the columns of wax, name by name, wick by wick, until he fell into a fitful slumber. Every night he studied them meticulously, like a general cataloging his arsenal, while his own weapon chugged and sputtered in his veins.

There was something not quite right about it now.

Halfway down the case, where the usual array of blizzards and snowstorms jostled for space between sunsets and sunrises, there was an almost imperceptible gap. Between *Saoirse*, which meant "freedom," and *Suaimhneas*, which meant "peace," *Spring Showers 2008* was missing.

Fionn crossed the room in three strides, jamming his feet into his sneakers without stopping to untie the laces first.

His grandfather peered after him, chomping on his sandwich. "Where are you off to in such a rush?"

Fionn shrugged his coat on and pulled his woolly hat over his ears. "There's been a theft!"

"Good grief. Of what sort?"

Fionn narrowed his eyes at his grandfather. "I think you know exactly what sort of theft I'm talking about. And thief too, come to think of it."

His grandfather smushed the rest of his sandwich into his mouth all at once until his cheeks swelled up like a blowfish and crumbs tumbled over his lips, then he pointed at his own face as if to say, I *can't talk right now, my mouth is suddenly very full.*

Fionn swung the front door open, and winter gusted right through it, curling the dark strands peeking out from underneath his hat. "We're supposed to *save* them!" he said angrily, before slamming the door behind him and taking off down the garden path.

The gate swung open for him, and the shrubs, skeletal without their summer foliage, *click-clack*ed a goodbye. Outside, a canopy of clouds smothered the rising sun. Fionn could see the usual flock of ravens patrolling the headland, chasing the seagulls back out to sea. The icy wind whistled alongside him, drowning out their faraway shrieks. It cleared stones from the roadway and tipped the flowers in reverie as he wound down the headland toward the strand.

He saw the whirlpool first. There, in plain sight of anyone who bothered to look, was the Storm Keeper's magic, skipping and dancing along the shoreline. Water twisted round and round, seafoam flying from its edges like cream from a mixing bowl. The longer Fionn watched it, the taller it became.

He swung his legs over the wall and stalked across the sand. "Hey!" he shouted. "Stop that!"

Across the beach, his sister turned to face him. She kept one hand outstretched toward the whirlpool, the other clenched around a turquoise candle that was burning upside down, devouring itself from the inside out. "Hey, loser," she said, through a wide grin. "What are you doing down here?"

Fionn marched toward her. "I told you a thousand times, you're not supposed to waste the candles!"

"I'm *practicing*," she said, turning back to the ocean. Her ponytail whipped through the air behind her, the ends of her winter coat flapping in the wind. "Grandad said I could have it, so just take a chill pill."

"It's not up to Grandad; it's up to me!" Fionn yelled. "Blow it out!"

Tara's laughter soared into the air. "You're so *dramatic*!"

"Coming from the girl who held a candlelit vigil the night Bartley Beasley went back to the mainland!"

She threw him a withering glance. "I told you I'm not ready to talk about that yet!"

Fionn yanked her by the arm.

The whirlpool faltered.

"Get off me!" Tara barked, shaking him off. "I'm concentrating!"

"The sun's almost up! Anyone could see you out here!" He glanced over his shoulder to where an old woman in a gray shawl was pottering along the strand. "See," he hissed.

"Don't be so paranoid," said Tara, not bothering to look. "You're *always* down here. You're just afraid the islanders will see how much better than you I am at this. How the waves actually *listen* to me. And then they'll start to wonder about *your* magic. Why they've never *seen* it. *Oooh.* The Storm Keeper's sister—maybe they'll say the island should have chosen me." Her lip curled in amusement, knowing she had touched a nerve. "Maybe they're right."

"*No*," said Fionn quickly. "You're just an idiot who's going through our stash of weapons faster than a bag of Skittles, because you're incapable of thinking of anyone but yourself!" He took a shaky breath. "If you didn't have less than ten brain cells, you'd *realize* that."

Tara stuck her chin out. "I have *loads* of brain cells. I always beat Grandad at Scrabble."

"Then prove it," said Fionn, glancing over his shoulder again. The old woman was gone. "Put it out."

"Fine." Tara crushed the remains of the candle in her fist and swung her free hand around until it was no longer facing the ocean but his face instead. In one icy deluge, the whirlpool leaped from the ocean and crashed over his head, soaking through his hat and pouring itself down his neck and into his clothes until streams of icy water gushed out of his pant legs, bleeding into puddles along the sand.

"Happy now?" she said, smirking at him.

Fionn glared at his sister, his words chattering violently through his teeth. "I wish, just once, we could bury *you* under a rock for all of eternity."

"Try it," she said, sashaying away. "I'd be back before the week was done."

Chapter Two

THE ROTTEN WAVE

An hour later, Fionn lingered outside Donal's corner shop, glowering into his hot chocolate. The sun had fought its way through the thicket of clouds, bringing an icy chill with it. It settled in the gaps between his toes and clung to the tip of his nose. All around him, fellow students milled by in scarves and hats and heavy winter coats, their bags *thu-thumping* against their backs as they chatted animatedly along the strand. It was the last day of school before Christmas and there was a giddiness in the air.

Fionn hardly noticed it; he was too busy staring at the marshmallow in his cup.

Do something. Anything.

He ground his teeth together, refusing to blink.

Give me a bubble. Just one little bubble.

His vision was starting to go funny.

Come on. Come on. Come on.

A horn sounded in the distance, making him jump. Fionn discarded his cup and rolled his neck around, blinking the tears from his eyes. Up ahead, the morning ferry was gliding into port.

He blinked again, this time in confusion. Not one ferry, but *two*—the second one following in the wake of the first.

Fionn frowned. In all the months he had lived on Arranmore, he had never seen one ferry so full, let alone two. He stepped out onto the strand and nearly crashed into the Aguero sisters. They divided around him, tossing identical veils of black hair in affront, as they made their way toward Fionn's sister, who was lingering outside the school gates. Tara caught his eye, then tapped her wrist, as if to say, *Hurry up, loser. You're going to be late.*

Fionn ignored her, turning instead in the opposite direction and tracking toward the pier. The boats were heaving with passengers. Most of them had spilled out onto the decks, where they stood shoulder to shoulder, like tightly packed sardines. When the second ferry horn blasted, they turned as one, suddenly standing to attention. There was something eerily familiar about it all—this strange sea of faces, moving silently across the water, each one marked by wide, unblinking eyes.

Soulstalkers.

Fionn stared in silent horror as the first boat docked. A wave rolled out from under it, swelling and frothing as it galloped toward the beach.

It brought a shoal of rotting fish with it. There were so many that Fionn could hear them splatting against the sand from where he stood up on the strand. He could even see their fleshy insides, their gloopy eyes and tarnished scales piling up and up and up, with every towering wave that came after.

Down on the beach, someone screamed. Douglas Beasley tore out of the post office with a parcel under his arm and Donal appeared in the doorway to his shop, his hair floating about his head like a cloud. Up by the school, teenagers discarded their conversations and craned their necks in curiosity.

The rotten waves kept coming, dead fish filling the air with a putrid, clinging stink.

Fionn clapped his sleeve over his mouth to keep from gagging, but he could do nothing about the accompanying panic. It rose up in his chest, pounding its fists against his heart until he felt like he couldn't breathe.

She had finally done it. Somehow, Morrigan had called

her followers home, and they had brought the shadow of death with them.

The thunder of nearby footsteps interrupted his rising hysteria. It came with his name, thrown up into the air like a football. "Hey! FIONN!"

Fionn snapped his head up to find his best (and only) island friend furiously sprinting toward him.

This was not usually the way of Sam Patton. Of the two of them, Sam was the unflappable one. He had seen so much more of the world than Fionn and was used to a less conventional life. It was what had drawn Fionn to him in the first place. That and the fact that Sam, despite growing up in London, was from one of the original five families of Arranmore. He had all but announced as much when he first alighted on Fionn in September, emerging from a gaggle of zombie-tired teenagers and stalking across the schoolyard with the confidence of a celebrity. "Storm Keeper!" He had scanned Fionn up and down, as though making sure of it. "You're a bit scrawnier than I expected but you do have a certain *look* about you. You remind me of my great-grandmother."

"Sam Patton," he had announced then, sticking out a leather-gloved hand. "Great-grandson of the one and only Maggie. She was a Storm Keeper too. I've been waiting to meet you all summer."

Sam was several inches shorter than Fionn, but his

sense of ease made him seem ten feet tall. He had big brown eyes, brown skin, and curly hair. It bounced along his forehead now, as he pelted along the strand, a flute case tucked under his left arm, the other flailing around him like a windmill. He skidded to a stop. "Look at the size of those waves!" he panted, before slapping his free hand over his mouth. "*Ugh*, that smell. It's getting *worse*."

The waves were still piling on top of each other, crashing and foaming as they painted the shoreline silver. "Where do you think they're coming from?" asked Sam, through his fingers.

"*Them*," said Fionn, gesturing at the pier. "It looks like Morrigan's minions have finally found her."

Sam turned on the heel of his boot. "Do you mean those passengers are—"

"Soulstalkers," said Fionn. "Can't you tell?"

Sam narrowed his eyes in suspicion. The first ferry was releasing its passengers onto the island. They scuttled across the pier like crabs, men and women dressed in scarves and coats and hats and suits, all moving in the same direction, one after another after another. "They don't blink," he said, with a shudder. "They just sort of *stare*."

"I *told you* something was coming." Fionn's insides were twisting and twisting. "I've been saying it for weeks now."

Tick-tock, tick-tock, tick-tock.

Morrigan hadn't been bluffing; she'd been gloating.

Sam shuffled uncomfortably. "Is this really an I-told-you-so moment?"

"I suppose not." Fionn swung his schoolbag around and pulled out his notebook. "Come on. We don't have much time. Let's get out of here before the beach fills up." He tucked it under his arm and gestured for Sam to follow as he stalked off up the strand and right past the school gates.

They left the bell ringing into the sky behind them.

"Ms. Cannon's bringing pies in today," said Sam, looking forlornly over his shoulder as he hurried to keep up with Fionn's determined strides. "They're my favorite."

Fionn passed the notebook to him. "If you help me save the island from oblivion, I'll make you a batch myself," he promised.

"I'm holding you to that," said Sam, slowing down to open the notebook. "And I want gingerbread men too. *With* buttons."

"Fine. Just read, please."

On the first page, Fionn had numbered and annotated the five Gifts of Arranmore in his messy scrawl. Sam read them aloud as they walked.

"One—**The Storm Keeper of Arranmore: to wield the elements in Dagda's name.** You said, '*Aka me. See also: useless.*'"

Fionn nodded grimly.

"Two—**The Sea Cave (earth): for that which is out of reach.** '*Used that one on Tara already. Very ungrateful.*'"

"Understatement," muttered Fionn.

Sam continued. "Three—**The Whispering Tree (fire): for that which is yet to come**. Says '*Probably should sort out the present before I go snooping around the future.*' Yep. Let's stay focused here.

"Four—**Aonbharr the Winged Horse (wind): for danger that cannot be outrun.** '*Might get in a bit of trouble if I fly away from the island by msyelf and leave it to die?*' Wow, Fionn. You think?

"Five—**The Merrows (water): for invaders that may come.**

"Ah yes, the terrifying mer-people of Arranmore," said Sam, before reading out Fionn's note. "'*This looks like the only option that can help us.*'"

"I'm afraid it is," said Fionn.

Sam *hmm'd.* "But the merrows are *way* scarier than mermaids. What if they eat us?"

"What if they *help* us?"

After a moment of contemplation, both boys trudging up the headland in silence, Sam slammed the notebook shut. "Right, then," he said, adjusting the lapels of his blue peacoat. "The merrows it is."

Fionn didn't miss the quiver in his friend's voice.

Merrows. Fionn had heard a dozen stories of the fin-tailed, blue-skinned mermaids that patrolled the deep waters of Arranmore. According to Fionn's mother, in the evenings, when lips were loosened, talk in the pubs would often turn to the sea creatures and their fabled barbarism, their shark-toothed mouths. There would be whisperings of sightings along the coast, mistaken seals and friendly dolphins re-embroidered with new details, the locals surrendering their tales like counterfeit coins. Fionn swore he had seen one once, buried in the folds of the ocean. He had felt something in his chest, a thread of magic going taut between them, but she was gone before he reached her.

"Is it a terrible idea?" he asked now.

"Not necessarily," Sam reasoned. "They'd certainly be helpful in the present . . . situation. Terrifying and hair-raising and guaranteed to give us nightmares for *years*, but definitely helpful. There is one small problem though . . ."

"We have no clue how to find them?" guessed Fionn.

"Pretty much," said Sam, with a shrug.

Fionn set his jaw. He had been anticipating this. "I think I know where we can start."

Chapter Three

THE SORCERER'S SHELL

Fionn led Sam all the way up the headland, where they slipped past *Tír na nÓg*, Fionn's grandfather's cottage, and continued north. The sea faded at their backs and the trees welcomed them into their fold, the evergreens bending their branches back and sprinkling pine needles into Fionn's hood.

After a while, they passed into the untamed heartland of Arranmore and found themselves approaching the edge of a lake. It squatted stagnantly beneath the island hills, their silver crests bunched together like a crumpled duvet.

"Here we are," said Fionn triumphantly.

"H*mm*," said Sam, staring skeptically at the lake. It was

the exact color of soapy dishwater. "If I'm honest, I was expecting a slightly better plan."

"Cowan's Lake is where Dagda made the very first merrow," said Fionn, pointing somewhat unnecessarily at the wide expanse of water. "It's an island legend."

"Trust me, I know all about this place," said Sam, setting his schoolbag down on a rock and laying his flute case gently on top. "My sister pushed me in last winter. I definitely got frostbite in my baby finger, but Mom says it's always been a bit stubby and that it's not okay to sue your own family members. Plus, Una's fifteen, so I'd be suing my parents, and what's the point of that? They're stretched thin with the kitchen renovation, and Dad's not had a great year *creatively*," he said, making air quotes. "He's only written four poems, and they're all about our cat. Anyway, what I'm trying to say is, this lake is *freezing*."

"But it's *also* magical," said Fionn. "Grandad says when Dagda made the first merrow, the lake was so full of raw magic that it lit up with every color imaginable."

"That's why the fish all look so stylish," said Sam with a grin. "They got their rainbow scales from Dagda."

"And then he just knelt in the water and pulled out the merrow, like she had been under there all along waiting for him," Fionn went on, shaking his head in disbelief. What *power* Dagda must have had to craft a creature from nothing but water. "*Lír*, he called her. It means 'of the sea.'"

"*Yeah* . . . ," said Sam slowly. "And then Dagda dumped our good friend Lír in the Atlantic Ocean and she *swam away* from Arranmore to make more of herself in the undersea. That all happened over a thousand years ago . . ." He raised an eyebrow with perfect precision. "You're not expecting to find another one hiding in here, are you?"

Fionn dropped his schoolbag onto the grass with a ceremonious thud. "I don't know," he said truthfully. "I thought it might be worth a look."

He didn't surrender the second morsel of truth—that this was the best and, crucially, *only* plan he had come up with in all these months of defunct magic.

They peered over the waters of Cowan's Lake. Unlike Sam, Fionn had never visited the lake before, though he knew it well enough from his mother's stories. It was the setting of rare summer days where she picnicked with her family as a child, flew kites and threw rugby balls, cannonballed and penguin-dived, long before her brothers moved to Chicago and forgot her. It was the place she and Fionn's father stole away to when they were teenagers, taking secret strolls in the reedy mulch, their school uniforms bunched up around their knees.

It was in this spot where, years later, Fionn's father had

gotten down on one knee with his grandmother's ruby ring and asked his mother to marry him. It was the Arranmore of their wedding photos, Fionn's mother's dress whipped about her like a floating meringue, his father's eyes as blue as the lake at his back.

"No offense, but if there was an ancient sea barbarian hiding in this lake, I *think* someone would have noticed it by now," said Sam, interrupting his reverie. "I reckon we'd have better luck in the ocean."

"They don't come when I stand on the shore and call for them," said Fionn with a frustrated sigh. "I've tried and they don't answer. They're *so* . . ."

"Shy?" said Sam. "Self-involved?"

"*Negligent*."

Yet Fionn refused to believe the merrows were gone for good. For his magic to be useless was one thing, but for the other gifts of Arranmore to desert him was quite another. He would not admit defeat so easily. "Grandad says sometimes the lake shows you visions if you're patient." He dropped to a squat. "He says it remembers things. *Magical* things."

"Yeah, like Storm Keepers," said Sam, with a trill of excitement. He knelt down beside Fionn. "Two summers ago, I saw Ferdia the Dolphin Rider *and* Patrick the Story Weaver in the same day." He fisted his fingers in the damp grass. "You should button your coat properly. Maybe fix your hair. It might be recording you right now."

"Patrick's my mom's favorite Storm Keeper," said Fionn. "He founded the Arranmore library."

"Mine's Lorcan the Wise, or maybe Maggie the Wave Sweeper. The best legend is definitely the one with the Fin Whale." Sam grinned. "They're both Pattons, obviously."

Fionn glanced sidelong at his friend. "What about Bridget the Cunning?"

Sam recoiled. "Don't be daft. She's a Beasley!"

Fionn chuckled to himself as he bent over the lake.

"My dad thinks Róisín, First and Fearless, was a Beasley, you know. Can you imagine? The *original* Storm Keeper. A Beasley! All raven hair and emerald eyes," said Sam dreamily. "He's written loads of poems about her."

"Yeah," said Fionn, a little distractedly. He was searching the lake for a different pair of eyes. A wide, yellow gaze, to be exact. Not a Storm Keeper, but a merrow hidden somewhere in the ancient ripples. Anything that might point him in the right direction. "Róisín's my grandad's favorite too."

The lake was lapping against the tip of his sneakers, but there was no sign of anyone in the gray water.

"Nothing here but memories, mate," said Sam, after a while. "I don't think we're going to find our merrow."

"I suppose it was a long shot." Fionn traced his fingers

in the icy water. His hand went numb immediately, but his chest grew warm. His magic was pricking its ears up. Just below the surface, streaks of color shimmered in and out, the bellies of colorful fish turned up in greeting.

"*Look*," gasped Sam. "The rainbow trout never come to the surface. They must like you!"

Fionn's magic flared in recognition of Dagda's fingerprints—here, still, after so much time had passed.

He watched the glowing fins until they shifted out of focus and he caught sight of himself: ashen skin and red-rimmed eyes. The water flickered, his reflection winking in and out, and suddenly there was a different face shimmering in the lake. It was pale as a winter sky, and dwarfed in an unruly bright red mane. Fionn was seized by the fleeting fear that it was Ivan coming up through the depths of time. But *it couldn't* be—there was no beard or crawling black tattoos, just a short, round nose and a wide, curving mouth.

"It's Hughie Rua, the pirate slayer!" said Sam giddily. "We have a painting of him at home! He's one of yours. A McCauley, like your mom! Must be why he's come up."

Fionn stared at the red-haired Storm Keeper as he opened his wide mouth and laughed with his teeth and his tongue and his tonsils, his shoulders moving in time with the ripples.

Fionn's magic somersaulted inside him, the heat in his chest blazing a trail through his entire body. He plunged the rest of his arm into the water. The fire climbed up his throat. Another minute like this and he felt sure he could open his mouth and breathe it across the lake like a dragon.

"Careful!" warned Sam. "You might fall in."

The water blinked, and a new reflection appeared. It was much wider than the first, painting itself all the way across the surface.

There was an almighty gasp. Fionn couldn't tell whether it belonged to him or Sam, only that somewhere, in another world, Dagda was standing on the banks of the same lake. He was as tall as Fionn remembered, his snow-white hair cascading over his shoulders. By his feet an emerald glinted, its underside wedged into a gnarled wooden staff. In his arms he held a writhing blue body—webbed hands and webbed feet, a long neck slashed with gills, and wide, yellow eyes rolling in their sockets.

"*Lír!*" Fionn plunged his other arm into the vision, until the lake tickled the underside of his chin.

Dagda laid the merrow down and bent over the water, his brow furrowing as he searched for something beneath the lake's skin. He came close enough that Fionn could see the trouts' glowing bodies reflected in his eyes, the thin coils in his cloudy beard.

The sorcerer reeled backward, a look of triumph on his face, as he pulled something hard and shiny from the lake. He settled it in the palm of his hand, and from another world its glittering rims winked at Fionn. It was a conch shell. And it was *steeped* in magic. Fionn could taste it on the back of his tongue, sharp and zingy as a citrus fruit.

There was a sudden, sharp pull in his chest.

Mine.

He surged forward, grasping through the looking glass, as Dagda rolled back on his haunches and raised the shell to his lips. Fionn's knees gave way, his weight tipping too far forward. Sam lunged for him and lost his balance, both boys yelping as they fell headfirst into the reflection, shattering it into a thousand bubbles.

They were yanked backward, saved from fully falling in by the hoods on their coats. Fionn coughed, and a mouthful of lake water trickled down his chin. Sam loosened the button around his neck and gasped at the air.

There was a new face glaring at them from the lake. They looked up over their shoulders to find an old woman standing on the bank behind them. Her fingers were still twined in their hoods. "You're welcome," she said, releasing them.

Fionn's hair was dripping down his face. The top half of his coat was stained four shades darker and the sleeves were welded to his skin. Dagda's reflection was gone, along with every lick of magic that had set his bones on fire. He felt as cold and gray as the lake before him.

He sighed, empty again. "Thanks."

The woman scowled at him. "You're running out of time."

Fionn and Sam exchanged a bewildered glance.

The old woman pointed skyward, to the weak sun. "The winter solstice casts night across the land like a shadow. When the light is weakest, dark magic is at its most powerful."

Fionn rolled onto his feet. "What solstice?" he asked warily. "What are you talking about?"

"Timing is *everything*." She was already moving away from them, toward the trees, her shawl pulled tight around her face. "There are no merrows here, only memory. And not the kind that might help you." Her last words drifted over her shoulder, carried on a harsh winter breeze. "Tick-tock, Storm Keeper."

Fionn gaped after her as she slipped between the trees. "*Who on earth* was that?"

Sam pushed a sopping curl out of his eyes. "That was Rose, from over the hill," he said, coming to Fionn's side. "She's a bit crazy. Plays bridge with my grandmother on Sundays."

Rose. Fionn was sure he had heard that name before,

but he couldn't catch the memory it belonged to. It was a firefly, flitting in a jarful of competing thoughts.

Timing is everything.

"I need to go home and talk to my grandad," said Fionn.

Sam nodded thoughtfully. "Honestly, you probably should have done that first. It's a lake, not the Bat-Signal. It was never going to solve this mess for us."

"Thanks for that," said Fionn sarcastically.

Sam only grinned at him, a dimple pressed into his right cheek. "You're welcome."

* * *

Fionn's grandfather was sitting at the kitchen table when he slipped back into the cottage, damp from head to waist. "Well, well, well . . . If it isn't Aquaman."

Fionn eased the door closed behind him. "Please don't tell Mom I didn't go to school," he said, hopping from one foot to the other to warm up. "She'll kill me."

His grandfather raised his brows over the rim of his mug. "Calm down, Riverdance. I'm no snitch."

"Thanks," said Fionn, shrugging his sodden jacket off.

"Were you out chasing dolphins?"

Fionn flung his schoolbag into the corner. "Merrows, actually. There's been a . . . development."

His grandfather set his mug down.

Fionn dropped into a kitchen chair and told him everything that had already happened that morning, from the mass arrival of dead-eyed Soulstalkers right up to why ice crystals were now hanging from the ends of his hair. His grandfather listened with practiced impassivity, a muscle feathering in his jaw when Fionn told him of Rose and her warning.

Timing is everything.

"The winter solstice," his grandfather muttered. "That's December the twenty-first. The longest night of the year."

Fionn stiffened in his seat. "The *twenty-first.* But that's only three days away!"

Tick-tock, crumbling rock.

Three days, watch the clock.

"The countdown!" Fionn leaped to his feet. "They're going to bring her back, Grandad. That's why they're here. Now that Morrigan's finally awake, they're going to raise her on the winter solstice!"

Fionn's grandfather dragged his hands across his face. "The winter solstice is a time of darkness and ritual. Morrigan's magic will be strongest then." He shook his head ruefully. "You're right, lad. It's no accident the Soulstalkers are here now."

Fionn said nothing. He was waiting for a flicker of his grandfather's trademark optimism, a wisecrack or a witty comment, even just a half smile to ease the tension.

"I'm sorry, lad. I should have predicted this." His grandfather closed his eyes and tipped his head back, releasing a sigh that seemed to go on and on and on. "I'm afraid you were right. We're almost out of time."

Chapter Four

THE BEACHED WHALE

Fionn's grandfather was waiting in the sitting room when Fionn got out of the shower. He was wearing his brown winter coat and stripy green scarf, his favorite flat cap already settled on his head. He greeted Fionn with his most mischievous smile, as though their previous conversation had never happened.

Fionn was still towel-drying his hair. "What's going on?"

"Your mother will be home from the library soon. Hurry up and get dressed. I've had a genius idea while you were showering." Then he marched toward his bedroom with the purposefulness of a drill sergeant, clapping his hands as he went. "Chop-chop, lad! Time waits for no one."

He chuckled under his breath, before adding, "Except me, of course."

Fionn got dressed at lightning speed, hurrying into his grandfather's room, only to find him nose-deep in his wardrobe.

"Just a second, lad," he said, in a muffled voice. "I know it's in here somewhere."

His grandfather's bedroom was as chaotic as ever. The wardrobe was wide open, with shirts falling from their hangers and ties spilling out of their drawers. His stacks of books had doubled in size since the last time Fionn had snooped around in there. The same floral curtains were pulled back in neat little loops, and beneath them, his grandfather's private collection of candles was lined up like straggling soldiers—the few and the special.

There were only four left now. With the absence of *Record Low Tide 1959*, which had seen Fionn nearly splattered on a rock during the summer, and *Cormac*, which had sent a fissure right through his heart, the shelf seemed particularly paltry. Beside *Record High Tide 1983* was the star-sprinkled *Perseid Meteor Shower*. Next was *Blood Moon*, which was shaped like an orange and dyed a vivid, fire-engine red. The last candle was fluorescent green, winding itself into an intricate spiral, before ending in a pointed silver wick. *Aurora Borealis*. The Northern Lights.

Fionn picked it up and rolled it in his hands. His chest grew warm almost immediately, his cheeks prickling as his magic cracked an eye open. "This one must be full of magic," he muttered.

His grandfather turned from where he was rustling inside his wardrobe. "There isn't a single candle in this cottage that I would keep from you, lad. Except that one."

At Fionn's look of confusion, he added, "That was the night your grandmother died."

"Oh," said Fionn, handing it straight back to him. "Sorry. I didn't know."

His grandfather traced the green spirals with his index finger, his wardrobe search momentarily forgotten. "The sky was brushed through with purples and greens so vivid it seemed like they were dancing along the Milky Way," he said quietly. "I came home late from the lifeboats and Winnie was outside in her chair, her beautiful face tipped back to the beautiful sky. It would have taken anyone's breath away . . ." He trailed off, staring too hard at the wax. "I thought she was sleeping."

Fionn swallowed. "Oh," he said again quietly.

His grandfather raised his head. "When it's my time to go, I'm going to burn this candle and find my way back to her." His smile was small, but there was a quiet kind of certainty behind it. "If the island allows me, I'll sit beside her under that same shimmering sky and we'll go together."

Fionn remembered what his grandfather had once told him, *fadó fadó*—long, long ago. *You can die in any layer of Arranmore. They're all as real as each other.*

His grandfather set the candle back on the shelf. "It wouldn't be useful to you anyway, lad . . . It's just the other half of this old man's heart."

"It must be very big," said Fionn. "You could never tell any of it was missing."

"That's because you're distracted by my rugged good looks." He winked at Fionn over his shoulder, gathered all the strands of his grief, and straightened up until he suddenly seemed much taller than before. "Now come on, we didn't come in here to wallow about things we can't change. We came in here to solve a problem."

He turned back to the wardrobe and dived in headfirst, flinging old shirts over his shoulder and whistling to himself as he rifled through shelf after shelf. Finally he removed a small shoebox from the back of his sock drawer and tipped its contents out. Nine candles, varying from deep blue to lilac gray, tumbled onto the bed.

"Just when I think I've seen them all," muttered Fionn. "This place sprouts more of them."

"Dolphin days, and the like!" said his grandfather

triumphantly. "These memories brought particular aquatic delights with them . . ." He poked at the candles with his finger, rolling them around to check their labels. "I inherited most of them," he told Fionn. "Winnie and I used to burn them on your dad's birthdays when he was a young lad. Cormac loved watching the dolphins . . . These ones I suppose he grew out of." He smiled sadly. "It's such a shame when children grow up. They become so moody and serious."

Fionn looked through the candles, his fingers drawn to a fat gray one, with deep, white ridges. He plucked it from the litter and raised it to his nose.

"*Ugh*." It was surprisingly pungent—a smell and a taste both at once. There was a distinct whiff of fishiness—salmon and mackerel and trout soaked in acid and bile, all fermenting together in a cooking pot. Then came the blubber—oil-slicked and swollen with salt. "This one does not smell like a dolphin," said Fionn, without having the slightest idea what a dolphin smelled like.

His grandfather's eyes lit up as he swiped it from him. "There it is!"

He held it up to the window, double-checking the label. "*Míol Mór*," he said, leaping to his feet and marching from the room. "Let's get our skates on, lad."

Fionn ran after him. "To where?"

"To the day the whale washed up!" His grandfather plucked a dry coat from the stand by the door and threw it at Fionn. "This candle contains the last known sighting of a merrow, Fionn. Muiris Beasley told anyone who would listen that he saw one watching them from the beach that day. Emily Patton wrote a short story about it years later and sent it to *The Times*. Didn't credit Muiris though. Big hullaballoo at the time," he said, striding out the door. "It was all my mother talked about for weeks. She used to say the Beasleys would bicker with their own reflections if they were left alone long enough. Then the Pattons would go away and write about it. *Anyway*, what do you say we get down to the beach and see if we can find that merrow?"

"I'd say it's the best plan we've got," said Fionn, slipping into his grandfather's old coat and following him outside. They joined hands under the clear sky. The front door shut behind them and the gate flung itself open. Fionn's grandfather held the candle out, and Fionn grabbed a lighter from his pocket and flicked it open.

He stopped abruptly as common sense caught the tail of his excitement.

"Wait," he said, his hand hovering above the candlewick. "Are you sure this is a good idea?"

Fionn wasn't eager to plunge into the past by himself, but he had seen firsthand how dangerous it was to anchor his grandfather to a different memory—especially one that would come and go with the wind. "I mean, for you to come with me," he added awkwardly.

His grandfather stared at him. "Well, obviously not," he said, jabbing the wick into the flame. "But when has that ever kept me from an adventure?"

And just like that, the wind was at their backs, kissing their cheeks and tugging their sleeves. The island dissolved, and a new one rustled into being. Afternoon skies gave way to morning blush as the headland stretched out before them. They walked, and then they jogged, and then they ran, and Fionn remembered what an island spinning on a magical axis felt like when it whipped by you.

"I've missed this," yelled Fionn's grandfather, waving the candle back and forth at the changing sky. An endless sheet of sapphire blue snapped into place, and a blazing sun climbed up its seam.

Fionn loosened the buttons on his coat as he ran. "I think we're a bit overdressed though!"

The grass was emerald green again, and full of purple flowers—the same ones that had winked in and out at him during his first few days on the island. "Look!" he said, as they disappeared under his feet and resprouted by the roadside, waving at him as they went by. "They're saying hello!"

"Forget-me-nots," said his grandfather, slowing to stroke one. It turned its face to him, its petals unfurling in plumes of violet. "They come and go as they please—just like us!"

Fionn bent down to do the same, but the flower ducked and then disappeared.

"Tricksy little beggars." His grandfather chuckled. "You can tell why they were your grandmother's favorite flower!"

The island was slowing down. Trees exploded with summer foliage, while thrushes swept down from the sky and chirped in greeting. Carts and horses clopped by, islanders in open shirts and shorts milling by them unsuspectingly.

The beach came upon them in a swell of activity. There was a crowd gathered down by the shore, women in cotton dresses and men in straw hats chatting animatedly along the strand. Children weaved in and out between them, laughing and skipping, while others pressed their faces to their mothers' skirts, too afraid to look.

Fionn and his grandfather hopped over the wall. The wind came along, prodding them further into the memory.

This way. Over here.

They took a wide berth of the crowd, sloshing through the shallows in their socks and shoes, the warm water threading cockleshells into their laces. Sea-foam climbed up Fionn's ankles but his eyes were glued to the spectacle before them. Without the wall of shoulders and craning necks, it unfolded like something from a storybook. There, on the Arranmore strand, under a cloudless sky, a gigantic whale had beached itself along the waterline.

Fionn's grandfather let out a low whistle. "Dagda's *beard*! Look at the *size* of that thing."

The *thing* was a marvel—a fully grown whale, bigger than the island's largest lifeboat. The gray-black of its hide was slick with ocean spray, its tub-like mouth opened to reveal its fleshy insides. Fionn could have climbed right in, curled up on its pink tongue, and still had room to toss and turn.

Along the sand, the locals were sporting matching shades of wonder. The sheer mass of the whale had cowed them, and as they stood in animated curiosity, the creature let out a keening groan that shook the earth beneath their feet. The air from it wafted such a stink that Fionn had to pinch his nose closed. The onlookers peeled backward, and a little girl at the front threw up onto the sand.

"That's your grandmother," said Fionn's grandfather, smiling fondly at the swaying girl as she was carted away by protective parents.

Fionn tore his gaze from the beach as they circled the mammoth beast, daring to step where no one else would. "Poor thing." He reached out to trace its ridges. "I think he's scared."

"Don't touch him," warned his grandfather. "If you mess too much with the memory, the island will kick you out."

"But he's frightened." There was something about this creature—ancient and indestructible, now stranded in its helplessness—that frayed the edges of Fionn's heart.

The whale jerked its flipper; it flapped against the damp sand. Spurts of seawater misted from its blowhole, while the waves lapped uselessly at its underbelly. The tide was giving up on him.

"I'm sorry," said Fionn, looking into his glassy eye. "We can't help you."

The crowd on the beach parted suddenly. A tiny woman with impossibly long dark hair was crossing the unseen line in the sand. She came right up to the whale, an arm's length from where Fionn and his grandfather were standing in the shallows, and bent down to look the creature in the very same eye. The wind whipped a strand of her hair into Fionn's face—and the smell of lavender tickled his nose.

He stumbled backward, startled.

His grandfather smirked. He had been silent for

so long, Fionn had assumed it was a consequence of his sadness at the whale's misfortune, but now he wondered whether it was simply the quiet confidence of someone hearing a story for the second time and already knowing the ending.

A hush had fallen over the beach. The crowed leaned closer, teenagers on tiptoes and children on shoulders to see what the diminutive woman was going to do. Fionn's grandfather squeezed his hand, and they moved backward into the waves. "Give her room, lad. Let her work."

Fionn stared at the woman as she stood before this prehistoric beast, her narrow shoulders squared to the wild Atlantic way. Her face was unlined, her skin tanned and freckled from years of sun. She was young, but her eyes were ancient. They were silver-gray, the same color as the wax dripping over his grandfather's fingers.

She smiled and a flicker of recognition lit up inside Fionn.

"That's Maggie Patton," he gasped. "The Storm Keeper before you!"

She was wearing Sam's toothy smile. It was a peculiar thing, Fionn thought, to be fashioned from secondhand parts, quirked mouths and big noses and high foreheads passed down from generation to generation, like gold earrings and well-worn watches.

"It was no small thing to gaze upon the power of Maggie Patton," said his grandfather approvingly. "Wave Sweeper, we called her."

"This is Maggie and the Fin Whale!" said Fionn, with a jolt of gleeful understanding. "We're standing in the middle of an island legend!"

His grandfather pointed to himself. "Yes, and you're standing next to one too."

All at once the sea began to bubble.

Maggie Patton threw her arms out wide, a cry springing from her as she raised the ocean like a blanket. Up and up it went, deserting crabs and oysters and shells and sprats, tangles of seaweed and shining rock, fish flapping against the solid sand. She flicked her wrist—a movement so small, Fionn barely caught it—and the water thinned to a wide silken sheet, leaping over the whale and scooping it up.

The whale was rolled onto its front, streams of water gushing underneath its hide as the ocean tightened its grip.

Gasps rose with the whale as it was lifted from the beach. Pink laces of coral dripped from its fins, and strings of seaweed tumbled from its mouth. The sea rained down on Fionn and his grandfather as it swallowed up the creature, first its tail and then its fins, its throbbing white underbelly and deep ridges, and, finally, its wide, glassy eye.

Fionn waved it goodbye.

The water kept rolling, reversing the tide and pushing the waves back out to sea. Slowly their crests shrunk. The froth dissolved into gentle ripples as Maggie Patton twirled her hand, as though she was offering up a royal goodbye.

And then the whale was gone.

The beach erupted. The islanders surrounded their Storm Keeper as she staggered onto the sand and sagged to her knees.

"Is she okay?" asked Fionn, craning his neck to see.

"The Storm Keeper's power is finite," his grandfather reminded him. "The bigger the magic, the longer the snooze."

The islanders hoisted Maggie Patton up between them and carried her from the beach. "Wave Sweeper!" they chanted, over and over. Fionn was reminded, with alarming quickness, of his own searing incompetence. He couldn't even command a glass of water, and here was another Storm Keeper wielding the ocean like a ladle.

Wave Sweeper, they called her.

What would they call him? *Sea Fearer? Magic Barren?*

His grandfather was pulling him away. "Don't dwell on it, lad. That's not why we're here."

Fionn remembered then. They hadn't come for the whale; they had come for the merrow—and somewhere inside the patchwork of this memory was the glint of blue skin on clear water. He just had to find it before the candle ran out. They tracked to the edge of the beach, following the curving peninsula out into the sea.

They stood there for several minutes, craning their necks and scouring the water with close attention until—

"Look! There!" said Fionn. Just out to sea, behind a cluster of rocks, a pair of yellow eyes floated atop the water. "Do you see her?"

Beside him, his grandfather stiffened. "Aye, lad. I see her."

Chapter Five

THE BROKEN MEMORY

The merrow was watching the strand, where the revellers were herding Maggie Patton into the nearest pub. Even from a distance, Fionn recognized her face—a nose pinched sharp as a blade, a moon-white scar tracing the hard line of her jaw. On top of her head, wedged into her shorn hair like bolts, she wore a twisted crown of coral and bone.

"Lír," breathed Fionn.

"*Terrifying.*" The word seemed to slip from Fionn's grandfather.

Fionn tightened his grip. "I need her to see me. Let me hold the candle, please."

"Be careful of disturbing the memory too much,"

warned his grandfather as he handed it over. "You might only have seconds before the wind changes."

When Fionn's fingers closed around the candle, the wind cut through him. The memory stretched, allowing him to exist inside it. It was an additional gift from Dagda—unsought and unexpected—transferred the minute Fionn had pressed his hands against the sorcerer's back a thousand and more years ago. When Fionn held the burning wax against his fingers, he could be seen in every layer. Even for a Storm Keeper, this was unique.

Across the sea, the merrow turned her gaze on him.

"Hello!" Fionn called out, before nerves could steal his voice from him. "My name is Fionn Boyle. I'm the Storm Keeper of Arranmore!"

The memory flickered; the air wavered and then held, like a kite catching the wind.

The merrow drifted toward them. Her skin was blue as the ocean, with barnacles, pearly shells, and mollusks spattered across her torso.

"Go on, lad," said his grandfather. "Keep talking."

"The island . . . *my* island is under attack," said Fionn. "I'm from a time many years from now. And in that future, Morrigan is awake, and her followers have returned."

The merrow leaned her folded arms on their rock.

"The Raven Queen stirs," she said, peering up at Fionn, "to face a Keeper no older than a common carp."

Fionn could hear the swell of the sea in her words, the violent rush of water bubbling in her throat. He licked the dryness from his lips. "Have you ever seen her Soulstalkers? Do you know what they're capable of?"

The merrow bared her teeth, but Fionn couldn't tell whether it was a smile or a grimace—only that it brought a terrible coldness to his bones. "I know the Raven Queen's followers. I've killed my fair share. The more of them that band together, the greater the sickness that rides with them. They exist in a weakened, stagnant state until the day their leader returns. Only when their souls are unburied can they return to their true power—to strength and agility and violence, the likes of which *you* have never seen."

Her gills flared in warning. "With dark magic they were made. But with magic too they can be felled."

Her pupils were keen and bloated as she watched him. They traveled the length of Fionn's arms, to the hand clutching his grandfather's invisible fingers.

Could the merrow sense him? Could she tell they had no magic between them?

"There are only three days until the winter solstice. I need the merrows to help me get rid of the Soulstalkers before that. I can't find a way to reach you in my time,"

Fionn went on quickly. "So I need you to remember this conversation and bring your people back in my future so I can fix this mess."

The merrow stared at Fionn for five very long seconds. Then she threw her head back and released a laugh so shrill, Fionn and his grandfather both jumped.

"*Goodness*," muttered Fionn's grandfather.

"Why are you laughing?" Fionn demanded.

When the merrow only laughed harder, he kicked a strip of seaweed at her. She caught it in midair and crushed it between her teeth.

"You must do your part before we do ours, Keeper. *That* is the way of Arranmore." Her jagged teeth glinted as she chewed. "You *earn* the gifts before they yield to you."

"But I'm the *Storm Keeper*," said Fionn, with growing impatience.

The merrow spat the seaweed at him. "Then you should know we are not bound to *you*."

Fionn blinked. "What do you mean?"

"By Dagda's will, we are bound to the Tide Summoner."

Fionn glared at her.

The merrow glared back. "Does the Storm Keeper not know of the Tide Summoner? The shell borne of ancient magic and merrow blood? The very thing that links *my* people to *your* island?"

"You mean the big white conch one?" said Fionn, remembering the shell in Cowan's Lake—a thing so full of magic that its imprint had half drowned him. "The one Dagda pulled from the water the day he made you? I've seen it, actually."

The merrow narrowed her eyes. "Then go back to your time and blow it."

Fionn glanced sidelong at his grandfather.

"You'd better tell her, lad."

"I don't have the shell. I only *saw* it," said Fionn. "But I really don't have time to look for it right now. We're kind of on the clock."

The merrow's frown cut through Fionn like a knife. "We answer to the one who wields the Tide Summoner."

"Who is that?" said Fionn and his grandfather at the same time.

"Who had it last?" added Fionn.

The merrow's smile was worse than her frown—it was all shark teeth, too wide and too sharp. "Hughie Rua."

Fionn reeled backward. "*Hughie Rua!*"

"Hughie Rua McCauley hasn't walked these shores in nearly three hundred years!" said his grandfather, aghast. "Not since the pirate invasion of 1728!"

"How am I supposed to find the shell if its previous owner has been *dead* for centuries?" said Fionn. His chest was blazing hot, but he couldn't tell if it was the Storm Keeper's magic or the heat of his own frustration. The candle was burning low. "I can't go off on a treasure hunt when the island is in danger," he said desperately. "Isn't there some other way you can help me?"

"A message for the floundering Keeper," said the merrow, smiling savagely as she pushed herself off the rock. "And the world that rests on his shoulders."

She skimmed a song along the sea as she drifted away from them, the melody as wild and terrible as the sound of her voice.

Two fates bound by Dagda's *hand,*
One at sea and one on land.
Lay worthy hands upon the shell,
And breath becomes the ocean's knell.
The bond that takes a touch to make
Will not before a lifetime break.
Eight waves to call the tide,
On the ninth wave, the merrows ride.

"*Why* is ancient Arranmore so *obsessed* with rhyming everything?" muttered Fionn's grandfather. "Can't everyone just speak plainly?"

"Wait, please!" shouted Fionn, lunging forward. "I

don't have time for this! The Soulstalkers are already here!"

"If you are worthy, you will find the shell." The merrow disappeared in a final ripple, the waves folding over her as though she had never been there at all.

"Come back!" Fionn leaned over the clear water. "You have to help me!"

"Fionn. She's gone." His grandfather was tugging him back.

"Our fates are linked!" Fionn swore he could see a flash of something in the water. He plunged his foot into the sea and splashed it frantically. His anger surged, and the wind surged with him, whipping his coat behind him. "You have to help us! It's your duty!"

"Fionn!" his grandfather warned. "Be careful! We'll be thrown out of the memory."

Fionn was too panicked to listen.

"We're going to die!" He kicked the water. The waves grew bigger and angrier, crashing against their rock until they were soaked from head to toe. "We're all going to die and you don't even care!"

"*Fionn!* You're angering the island!"

The ground began to shake, as though the world was slipping out from under them. A gust of wind came down like a whip and tightened around Fionn. He screamed as he was torn from his grandfather's grip and thrown backward, landing on the rocks with a sharp thud.

The candle in his fist went out, the blackened wick crumbling to ash as the rest of the wax streamed over his fingers, warm and runny as blood. The sky churned, summer blue to angry clouds of gray and purple. The earth groaned, and a bolt of lightning stabbed the horizon.

He had taken it too far.

He had done too much to the memory, and it had kicked him out.

The second realization came a heartbeat later.

His grandfather was gone.

The wind tornadoed around Fionn as he flattened himself against the rock and spider-walked back to the beach. The sea sprayed salt in his eyes. The sky flickered, like pages flying through a sketchpad, the angry storm dissolving to lead gray and then winter white. By the time Fionn made it to the end of the peninsula, his hands were numb and his teeth were chattering, but he was too frightened to care. He sprinted along the empty beach as the island reset itself. "Grandad!" he yelled. "Grandad! Can you hear me!"

There was nothing but the howling wind.

"I'm sorry!" he shouted, not just to his grandad, but to the island too. "I'm sorry I got so angry! I'm sorry I messed with the memory!"

He tracked the entire beach twice, running and yelling, until finally the air hiccuped and Fionn's grandfather appeared before him.

He was standing alone by the water's edge.

"I'm sorry!" Fionn panted as he caught up with him. "I don't know what came over me. I wasn't thinking!"

He felt it before he saw it—the door that had slammed in his grandfather's mind, the bolt that had slid into place. His blue eyes had clouded over. "Cormac," he said, staring past Fionn into the distant sea. "The tide is awfully low, isn't it?"

"Yes," said Fionn, relief mingling with dread at his grandfather's confusion. "Yes, it's very low."

His grandfather frowned at the sea, as if he had lost something in its froth.

"Let's go home," said Fionn, taking him by the sleeve. "We can put the fire on."

"Did you see the dolphin, Cormac?" he said, following him across the sand. "I'm sure I saw something in the waves."

"No," said Fionn. "I must have missed that."

At the top of the beach, an old woman was watching them, her shawl arranged about her face so Fionn could see only the curious tilt of her head. Rose. She stood back to give them room as Fionn helped his grandfather over the low wall. His movements were stiffer now. When he reached the other side, he sat down heavily, his hands grasping his knees as he tried to catch his breath. "My legs are creaking," he panted. "I can hear them."

Fionn hovered in front of him like a barrier, all too conscious of prying eyes. "That's okay. So are mine."

His grandfather looked up at him. "I'm getting old, Cormac."

"At least you're still handsome."

"Aye," he said quietly.

Fionn helped him to his feet, looping his arm through the crook of his grandfather's elbow as they made their way up the headland, leaving Rose behind. "Are we going to see the dolphins, Cormac? We shouldn't leave your mother out. She'd be heartbroken."

"No, not today," said Fionn gently. "It's too cold."

He desperately wanted to talk about the Tide Summoner, about what Hughie Rua might have done with it before he died. But his grandfather was a million miles away now, in some forgotten place where Fionn was not Fionn at all, but Cormac, his father.

He sank into the role with depressing ease.

They walked up the hill in silence, Fionn's grandfather stopping every now and then to pluck forget-me-nots from the frosty earth. They popped up with surprising regularity, their heads bent in submission, as they were swept into his bouquet, one by one. "For your mother," he muttered, time and again. "Winnie loves these."

They trundled up the hill like that, plucking the same flowers and having the same conversation about dolphins and the cold, and the cold and dolphins, and dolphins and the cold, until the land flattened and the little cottage appeared before them.

Then, like the twist in a terrible movie, Elizabeth Beasley sprang up in the distance, marching toward them in an outrageous fur coat and matching hat. Fionn decided that the only thing more dreadful than encountering Bartley Beasley's grandmother in that particular moment, was encountering Bartley Beasley's grandmother decorated with twenty dead badgers and her famous simpering smile.

"Malachy Boyle," she called out. "Do my eyes deceive me?"

Fionn's grandfather blinked at her dumbly.

"Let's go a bit faster," said Fionn, pressing his palm against his grandfather's back. "I think it's about to rain."

Elizabeth slid in front of them, peering up at Fionn's grandfather as though he had appeared from thin air, a genie finally freed from his lamp. "What an unexpected *surprise*."

Fionn's grandfather frowned. "Who is this woman, Cormac?"

Elizabeth's eyes widened. "Cormac?" she said, looking

at Fionn with dawning alarm. "Don't you know your own grandson, Malachy?"

Fionn's grandfather blinked at her.

"What are you doing here, Mrs. Beasley?" said Fionn icily. He amplified his disdain twofold—once to draw her attention away from his grandfather, and twice because she deserved it. "Don't you live down by the bridge?"

With the other trolls, he added in his head.

Elizabeth glowered at him. "That's no tone for your elder, boy," she said, with equal frostiness. "I've come to see *you*, since you're not at school, where you're supposed to be. I'm surprised you have to be told at all, in fact. We never had to do this sort of thing with past Storm Keepers. Even your grandfather was good in his time."

"What sort of thing?" said Fionn, ignoring the jibe.

"As if we haven't had enough trouble dealing with all those disgusting dead fish this morning, now there's a whale washed up over on Aphort Beach. Douglas is down there as we speak."

Fionn went very still. "A whale."

"A whale," echoed Fionn's grandfather. "Have you told Maggie?"

"Maggie is long dead," said Elizabeth, her disdain momentarily softened by bewilderment. "For goodness sake, you were at her funeral, Malachy."

"What does it look like?" asked Fionn, suddenly breathless.

"I don't know," she said sharply. "A whale is a whale. It's big and ugly and it's upsetting the children. Do you want to start doing your job *at long last* and do something with it, or should I have Douglas deal with it?"

Panic rushed through Fionn like a wave. This was a test, and he was about to fail it. He couldn't do what Maggie Patton did with that whale, not in a million years.

"Some time this century, please, Fionn," said Elizabeth, tapping her foot impatiently. "The carcass is already stinking up the beach."

"C-carcass?" Fionn stammered. "You mean it's dead?"

Elizabeth frowned at him. "Well, of course it's dead. And if we're not careful it will explode, too. Then we'll have an even bigger problem on our hands."

Fionn caught his breath before it whooshed out of him. This was no coincidence—the Soulstalkers set foot on Arranmore, a shoal of rotting fish heralding their arrival, and now this: a dead whale. What else was coming? What other terrors would the days before the solstice bring if he didn't find a way to protect his island?

He needed a plan. He needed a *miracle.*

"A dead whale," said Fionn's grandfather, to himself. "That's going to upset your mother, Cormac. Bad luck for the island. Bad luck for everyone."

Elizabeth gaped at him. "What on *earth* has gotten into you, Malachy?"

"Can Douglas deal with it, please?" Fionn dodged around Elizabeth, pulling his grandfather by the sleeve of his coat. "Grandad isn't feeling well and I want to get him home."

"Who was that old woman?" said Malachy, looking over his shoulder as Fionn led him away. "I don't think I know any Russian oligarchs."

Elizabeth Beasley stared after them, with her mouth wide open.

Within seconds, Fionn's grandfather had forgotten the encounter completely.

The same, Fionn knew with unsettling certainty, could not be said of Elizabeth.

Fionn's mother was waiting for them inside the cottage. She turned at the sound of the front door opening, a half-peeled parsnip raised in accusation. "*There* you are," she said, glaring at Fionn, while simultaneously beckoning them in. There were chopped carrots by the sink, a basin full of half-peeled potatoes on the counter, and a chicken roasting in the oven. It bathed the little kitchen in a warm, delicious glow. "Shut the door and keep the heat in. Are you all right, Malachy? You look very pale."

Fionn's grandfather was already drifting into the sitting room. Fionn followed him inside and helped him slip off his wet shoes and socks as he sank into his favorite armchair. He was still wearing his buttoned-up coat and hat, and the bottoms of his pant legs were damp with seawater.

"Fionn."

"Yeah."

"Can you come in here, please?"

Fionn dragged himself into the kitchen to face his mother. She was leaning against the oven with her arms folded across her chest. "I've just had a visit from Elizabeth Beasley."

"I am sorry," said Fionn. "I wouldn't wish her on my worst enemy."

"Any particular reason you decided to skip school without telling me, and then go off gallivanting with your grandfather, who you know very well isn't supposed to be out and about, without leaving me any kind of indication where you might have gone?"

Fionn cleared his throat. "It was Storm Keeper business."

There was an awful stretch of silence. Fionn could feel his mother's gaze, like a fingerprint on his forehead. "What *sort* of Storm Keeper business?"

"The maritime sort?" said Fionn.

His mother frowned. "Is this about the dead whale over on Aphort Beach?"

Fionn sighed. "Sort of."

"Or the legion of Soulstalkers that arrived this morning," she added, in a steely voice.

Fionn blinked at her. "You saw them too?"

His mother tried to suppress a shudder but he could see it rattling behind her eyes. "I saw the boats through the library window. The temperature dropped by ten degrees in the space of a minute. I had to get the spare heater out of storage. Then I ran into Sonia Patton, who said Sam came home in the middle of school, half soaked and raving about merrows and a beachful of rotting fish. And now, this whale business . . ."

"I did *say* something was coming," said Fionn.

"Not to most of the island, you didn't." His mother shook her head. "You and your grandfather are much too secretive, Fionn. This is a problem we are *all* part of now, and sooner or later we are going to have to do something about it."

"Sooner than you think," muttered Fionn.

"Cormac!" called his grandfather, from inside the sitting room. "Can you put the kettle on?"

"I'll do it," said Fionn's mother. "Go and make a fire for your grandad, then come back here, peel the last of the potatoes, tell me exactly where you were, and I won't ground you." She smiled, but her eyes were still sad. The same as always. "Deal?"

"Deal," he said glumly.

Fionn set about lighting a fire, shoveling coal and sticks into the little grate, his fingers shaking all the while. He dumped in too many firelighters, struck a match, and prayed it would take. Then he went back to the kitchen to make tea.

He stirred it in a trance, mahogany turning to milky brown. Round and round the spoon went, the metal of it glinting like a merrow's fin.

We are bound to the Tide Summoner.

If you are worthy, you will find the shell.

Fionn's grandfather accepted his mug gratefully, setting it onto his lap, beside his bouquet of purple flowers. "Will you fetch your mother for me, Cormac? I have something for her."

"She's out right now," said Fionn, placing the fireguard in front of the grate and watching the candle on the mantelpiece with a familiar rush of resentment. "She'll be home soon."

When he turned around, his grandfather's eyes were closed. "Winnie," he whispered, a smile dancing on his lips. "Winnie, Winnie, Winnie."

Chapter Six

THE WARRIOR'S HEART

That night, Fionn stood before a gaping chasm and watched the darkness shift beneath his feet.

Everything dying and everything dead, a soul filled with fear and a heart sick with dread, came Morrigan's familiar, mocking voice. *Soon the sun will turn its back on you, and I will stretch the night around me like a shroud.*

Fionn dangled a foot over the chasm. The ground rippled, and a face formed in the darkness. He recognized the pallid skin and soulless eyes, the deep crimson hair, and a smile full of purpose.

Ivan.

Tick-tock, Storm Keeper.

Tick-tock, comes the Reaper.

Something prodded him in the back and Fionn stepped off the ledge, tumbling into the infinite blackness, where there were no names, no voices, no souls at all. He woke with a scream throbbing in the base of his throat.

The wind was howling down the chimney, wobbling the candles on the shelves. For once, Fionn welcomed the cold; it quelled the fire in his cheeks and filled his lungs with new breath. His hands were still shaking. He slid one under his pillow and clamped Dagda's emerald in his fist. It was perfectly round, and warm to the touch. It had been months since it followed him home from the Sea Cave, stowed away in the pocket of his jeans, and though it served no purpose in Fionn's life, he kept it close to him. It reminded him of the ancient sorcerer—that he'd existed, once. That he was powerful, once.

More powerful than *her*.

He turned the emerald over in his fist, studied the green glow in the half-light of the little sitting room.

Where are you?

And why aren't you helping me?

Slowly, softly, the wind died down, and Fionn's pulse settled in his ears.

He could hear someone already awake in the cottage. He sat up just as his mother burst through the sitting-room door. Her hair was piled in a messy bundle on her head, and she was wearing a woolly green cardigan over her checkered pajamas. "Get up," she said, shooing at him with her hands. "We have people coming, and I haven't showered yet. We need to get some cookies out and put them on a nice tray. And flick the kettle on, find some nice mugs. God, I hope we have some decent custard creams or gingernuts left. Your grandad is always scarfing them down when he thinks I'm not looking!"

Fionn rubbed the sleep from his eyes, blinked once at the dull sky outside the window and then once at his mother. "Mom, the sun's not even up properly. Who are you expecting so early?" he croaked in his morning voice, before thinking to add, "And *who* eats custard creams at breakfast time?"

"Can you put your things away in the bedroom?" she said, ignoring his question before turning around and yelling, "TAAAAAARA!"

Fionn winced.

A half second later, Fionn's sister trudged through the door, bleary-eyed and unkempt. "I'm here," she yawned. "I'm helping. I said I would."

"Helping with what?" said Fionn, looking between them.

His mother was clanging and banging her way through the kitchen, pulling out plates and mugs and dusty old cookie tins. "The meeting," she said, her head in the cupboard under the sink. "It was your sister's idea."

Fionn turned, very slowly, toward Tara.

She folded her arms across her chest. "Now, don't get mad . . ."

"I'm already mad," said Fionn, to save himself time.

"Last night, we had a long talk about your role in all this scary business, and we made a decision."

Fionn frowned at his sister. Yesterday evening he had told them everything he knew about the Soulstalkers, their plans for the coming solstice, and the two short days that separated them from Morrigan's rising. He had even confided in them about the merrow Lír's song and the elusive Tide Summoner, choosing to go against his gut and trust his sister instead of excluding her. And *this* was how Tara had repaid him . . .

"You made a decision about me without *consulting* me?"

"You were asleep," said Tara without blinking. "We decided that that old shell is a waste of our time and we're better off coming up with a proper strategy before we all get killed."

"But—"

"We decided to be *practical*," Tara interrupted. Fionn glared at his sister.

She plowed on determinedly. "We've called an urgent

island meeting to discuss the Soulstalker situation and prepare the islanders for what we're facing. The committee will be here in twenty minutes, so clean yourself up and try to look like you know what you're doing. It's not like you inspire confidence, even at the best of times."

Fionn stared at Tara while her words waded through the morning mist in his brain. "The *committee*," he repeated. "And who are they exactly?"

"Found the good tray!" called Fionn's mother from inside the kitchen. "Everyone can relax now!"

"Representatives from the other families," said Tara coolly. "And the non-descendants too. It's an *island* problem, after all."

"It's *my* problem," said Fionn. "I'm the Storm Keeper."

Tara whipped the blanket off him. "You've had enough time, Fionn."

"Hey!" he yelped, folding his arms around himself. "I didn't even *know* about the Tide Summoner until yesterday. That changes *everything*."

Tara didn't look at him; she just kept folding his blanket, smaller and smaller and smaller. "It doesn't change a *thing*, Fionn."

"Yes, it does!"

Tara dropped the blanket on the floor in a neat square.

"Tell that to the islanders who watched two more boatloads of Soulstalkers arrive late last night." She whipped the sheet off the couch cushions and balled it around her arms, faster and faster and faster. "You slept right through it." She dropped the scrunched sheet onto the folded blanket, then plopped his pillow on top. "The world still turns, you know. Even when you're sleeping."

"So you decided to go behind my back and take control of everything?" said Fionn, getting to his feet.

"I wouldn't *need* to go behind your back if you didn't insist on keeping everyone in the dark while you try to do everything yourself. Do you realize how *pigheaded* that is?"

"I'm not pigheaded," said Fionn. "This is *my* job, not yours. I told you about the Tide Summoner. I'm going to find it."

"Oh, don't be ridiculous," snapped Tara. "We don't have time for a wild goose chase!"

"*Fionn, Tara,*" warned their mother from inside the kitchen, where she was now bent double over the sink, trying to scrub a stubborn grease stain off the "good tray." "It's too early for bickering."

"*Glory hog,*" said Tara to Fionn. "You just want to be the next Hughie Rua. Do you think that was clever of him, sneaking out in his little boat and facing all those pirate ships alone? Do you think he was *brave* not to ask his own islanders for help, to not even *tell* them what was happening? To just *risk their lives* instead?" She swept her hand around. "You know what I think? I think it was all ego and arrogant stupidity!"

"Why would he panic the other islanders when he didn't have to? He wasn't *alone*. He had the Tide Summoner," said Fionn defiantly. "He stood up against those pirates with an army of merrows at his back, and that's exactly what I plan to do when I find the shell!"

Tara rolled her eyes. "Look. Do you want my advice?"

"Obviously not," said Fionn immediately.

"We only have two days left." She went on anyway. "That stupid shell is gone. It's been gone for *hundreds of years*, in fact. We have to find our *own* path."

"And what path would that be?" asked Fionn. "One *you* get to choose?"

"Well, it looks like only one of us is fit to," said Tara viciously. "Or did your magic miraculously start listening to you overnight?"

Fionn scowled at his sister. "What's it like living with the devil inside you, Tara? Does it get very warm at night?"

"Okay, that's enough!" their mother shouted through the archway. "Tara, go and get dressed. Fionn, move your stuff into the bedroom and fix your hair."

Without another word, Tara tightened her ponytail

and marched into the hallway, disappearing without a backward glance. Fionn stalked into the kitchen, where his mother was scrubbing her fingers raw. "Are you sure she's yours?" he asked her. "What if there was a mix-up at the hospital and you took home Lucifer's baby instead? It happens, you know. I read an article about it once."

"Fionn, you might be the Storm Keeper, but you're a McCauley too, and we don't speak to our siblings that way," said his mother sternly. "Even at our *worst*, my brothers and I always apologized to each other."

"Yeah, but did you hear what she said about—"

"It's an archway, Fionn, not a soundproof bunker." She placed the tray down with a dull thud and dropped the rag in the sink. "Tara's trying to help you, sweetheart. She's right about Hughie Rua. He went out against those ships all by himself, when he could have taught the rest of the islanders how to use those candles and let them help him. If it wasn't for the wind carrying him back to shore that day, he would have drowned by himself in the ocean." She dried her hands on the tea towel; they were blotchy and red, her thumbnail chipped down the middle. All for a stain Fionn couldn't even see. "He gambled their lives without giving them a choice . . ." Her voice was climbing; she swallowed the sudden shrillness. "He didn't have to go by himself. That's all we're saying."

Fionn suddenly knew exactly who his mother was thinking about—not Hughie Rua at all, but someone else who had gone out in a boat by himself, in a time much closer to theirs. Someone who hadn't had a choice. Someone who never made it home.

"Mom," he said quietly. "This isn't like that."

Fionn's mother pulled her cardigan tighter around her. "Your father did not leave this green earth so that we would hide under our beds and make you face those monsters alone. Your father—" Her voice broke unexpectedly. She stared too hard at the floor, a shadow moving behind her eyes.

"Mom," said Fionn. His heart was aching, his throat too. "It's okay."

"Arranmore people are loyal, Fionn," she went on. "They will help if you ask them to. No matter the odds. No matter the consequences. You don't have to carry this burden all by yourself, working magic or no magic." She stared at him with red-wired eyes. Fionn recognized that look—it came from sleepless nights and stress-filled days, hours spent in her own head, dwelling in secrets he'd never known. "Do you understand what I'm saying?"

Fionn nodded. "We're going to face this threat together."

"Yes, we are," she said, taking his hand and squeezing it tight.

Fionn saw it then for the first time in his life, though he supposed it had always been there, mired in rain clouds, beating its way through the darkness. His mother had a warrior's heart.

He hoped he had one too.

"Now, please move your bedding, and put the good throw over the couch. I will not have Elizabeth Beasley looking down her nose at us, impending doom or not." She slipped by him, unwinding her hair from its messy knot. "I'm going to shower. Get the door when it goes. And please, *be polite.*"

Fionn did as he was told, and even fluffed the cushions as a show of good faith to his mother, though if he knew where Elizabeth was going to sit, he might have slipped a pin in there.

As he finished, his grandfather appeared hesitantly around the door, whistling to himself. "Is it safe to come out yet?" he mock-whispered. "Or is she still giving everyone jobs?"

Fionn hugged a cushion to his chest. "Did you know about this secret meeting?"

"Aye."

"And you didn't try to *stop* it?"

"Stop it?" he said, his brows rising. "I encouraged it."

Fionn glared at him. "But the Tide Summoner—"

"Fionn." His grandfather raised his hand. "That shell is a fool's errand. We don't know a thing about it."

"So you're giving up on me then," said Fionn sourly. "You don't even want to consult me about island stuff anymore." Of all the people in this little house, Fionn would have expected his grandfather to include him in the decision to call the other families to *Tír na nÓg*, but he had been considered and found lacking while he slept, and that stung him more than anything his sister had already said to him that morning.

His grandfather removed his glasses and cleaned them on the corner of his blue sweater. "This is not me giving up on you, Fionn. This is me getting in your corner and standing with you. We can't wait any longer for your magic to behave. We're almost out of time, and the islanders need to know what's happening."

He slid his glasses back up his nose and looked at Fionn over the rims. "There is no weakness in knowing when to ask for help. There is *strength* in vulnerability and there is *strength* in numbers. And believe it or not, there are forces stronger than magic, lad." He tapped Fionn on his nose, smiling broadly. "But there is nothing so strong as a grandfather's love."

Fionn only glared harder at him. "You are not talking your way out of this one."

His grandfather sighed. "If it makes you feel any better, inviting Betty Beasley and her spawn into my house will be as painful for me as it will be for you."

Fionn folded his arms across his chest. "It had better be."

Chapter Seven

THE POET'S TALE

Elizabeth Beasley materialized on the doorstep at precisely 9 a.m., as if she had been summoned from a Ouija board. She pushed past Fionn into the warm glow of the cottage. "It's freezing out there," she said, as Douglas shuffled in behind her. "I'll have a tea. Milk, and three spoons of sugar."

She didn't say please.

By way of greeting, Douglas pointed over his shoulder and said, "Three dead robins in your garden, Boyle. You might want to see to that."

Then the Cannons came. Alva, who was both a teacher in Fionn's school and an old family friend, embraced Fionn's mother as if they hadn't seen each other in a hundred years, despite having had lunch together two days before. Her brother Niall had accompanied her. An old classmate of Cormac Boyle, he was the captain of the Lifeboat Crew now. He was suitably weather-beaten and stubbled—and looked to Fionn like he could scale the Arranmore Cliffs with his bare hands if he needed to. He smiled warmly at him as he slipped inside, ruffling Fionn's hair in a way that made him think of the father he had never known.

The Patton delegates arrived on the heels of the Cannons, and though they brought news of another two ferry-loads of Soulstalkers come to shore just that morning, Fionn was glad to see Sam traipsing into the cottage alongside his father. "No one else wanted to get up this early," he said with a shrug. "We're not morning people."

They found a sliver of space in the rapidly filling sitting room, Mr. Patton settling into a chair dragged in from the kitchen, while Sam wandered around the shelves, trailing his finger curiously along the candle labels.

Tom Rowan, a wily old sheep farmer from the heartland of the island, came on behalf of the non-descendants of Arranmore, a fresh package of cookies in one hand, "just in case," and his pitchfork in the other—just in case. Juliana Aguero hadn't been invited, but he had happened upon her in Donal's shop and revealed just enough to make her trail after him curiously all the way to Tír *na n*Óg. "I thought I'd better come too," she told Fionn gravely as he led them inside. "I owe it to my fellow students. I am a prefect, you know."

In the little sitting room of Tír *na n*Óg, the committee assembled themselves between endless shelves of candles, armed with tea and cookies and grim smiles.

"Well, here we all are," said Fionn's grandfather, who was sitting on the floor by the fireplace. "The Knights of the Round Sitting Room. It has quite a nice ring to it, doesn't it?"

"We are hardly *knights*, Malachy," said Elizabeth primly, from Fionn's grandfather's favorite armchair. She looked pointedly at Fionn when she added, "And we *certainly* have no Arthur. No leader at all, in fact."

"Proper order, Betty. That's our Storm Keeper you're talking to," said Niall Cannon, earning an impressed smile from Fionn's mother. "Fionn will lead if you give him half a chance."

"I've given him half a *year*," Elizabeth shot back. "And now the island is practically overrun!"

"This is a committee with a common goal." Alva slipped seamlessly into her teacher's voice—calm and measured, with just a hint of authority. "Let's not be nasty to each other."

"Let's not get *murdered*," said Douglas, who was standing stiffly by the window, blocking the morning light with his boxy shoulders. "How about that?"

Mr. Patton raised his mug. "Do you have a drop of whiskey for the tea, Evie?"

"Dad," hissed Sam. "The sun's barely up!"

"I'll have one too, if it's going," said Fionn's grandfather. "Hold the tea though."

"*Malachy*," snapped Fionn's mother. "Behave."

Fionn's grandfather raised a hand in surrender. "As you were, Evie."

"Yes, Evelyn," said Elizabeth. "You certainly look like you want to say something, which is surprising, quite frankly. It's been a long time since the McCauleys have bothered to involve themselves in island business, considering most of you emigrate every chance you get."

Fionn's mother leveled Elizabeth with a long, dark look. "Well, you have one standing in front of you now, Betty."

"Then say something," said Elizabeth coolly.

Fionn looked up at his mother. She was standing with her back to the fireplace, her arms folded across her chest.

"We've gathered you here this morning so that you might speak for your families and help us face a...

concern." She pressed the word between her lips. "As Betty *kindly* pointed out, our island is being overrun by Morrigan's followers. Hordes of Soulstalkers have already made their way back to Arranmore, and they continue to arrive with every ferry crossing. The island is suffering, and we need to do something about it."

There was a collective murmur of agreement.

"It's come on so suddenly," said Alva, shaking her head. "All those horrible rotting fish yesterday."

"And that awful *whale,*" said Douglas, with mustache-twitching disgust. "The *sight* of it would give you nightmares."

"My best horse is dying," announced Tom Rowan. "I found Clyde slumped in the ruins of the old McCauley house yesterday. West Nile virus, the vet says."

"But we're nowhere *near* Egypt," said Juliana, who was perched like a frightened bird on the edge of the couch. "It's miles away!"

"Well, obviously," said Elizabeth, in a bored voice. Of everyone in the little cottage, she alone had remained in her outdoor wear. She was swaddled snugly in her fur coat, her equally elaborate hat giving her the unmistakeable air of a *Titanic* survivor. "Why would the animals get off so easily? The Soulstalkers are affecting everything."

"Cowan's Lake is completely frozen over," said Alva. "I took the twins up there this morning for our morning walk."

"And I haven't been able to create in *months*," said Sam's dad, shaking his head. "*The Times* called my last collection 'barely memorable.' " He looked around the room in dismay. "Never in my *life* have I had to endure such—"

"Get ahold of yourself, Phil," snapped Elizabeth. "I hardly think your declining genius is a consequence of our invasion. Although I can see the convenience in lumping it into our pool of grievances."

Douglas snorted.

"Should we lump your arduous personality in while we're at it, Betty?" said Fionn's mother. "Because it certainly isn't helping us focus here."

Niall covered his smile with his hand. Fionn and Sam didn't bother to trap their amusement, choosing instead to laugh loudly and openly, for much longer than necessary.

"All Dad's roses died last night. There was nothing but thorns everywhere when we woke up," said Juliana, her dark eyes wide with fear. "They're ruining our land."

"And the tides too," said Douglas. "They're lower than I've ever seen them. Keeping to their own rhythm, and bringing dead things with them. The fishermen don't know what to make of it."

"It's peculiar all right," said Niall, hunching forward. "Last night, when the last ferry load came in, I followed the Soulstalkers across the island." He shifted his gaze from side to side, as though there might be watchers at the windows. Everyone leaned a little closer. Even Elizabeth's chair creaked in the silence.

"They moved like an army. They didn't pause once. I tracked them all the way toward the lighthouse, and then down by the cliffs. They got on their hands and knees and went right over the edge. I waited as long as I could, but they didn't come back up." He shook his head, a frown knitting his dark brows together. "Not one of them returned."

"So the creepy devils are hiding *under* the island," said Tom, sucking a breath through his teeth. "But to what end?"

Fionn and Sam exchanged a look. The same one passed between Fionn's mother and his grandfather, but it was Tara who spoke up.

"They're waiting for the winter solstice. On December the twenty-first, Morrigan's magic will be at its strongest. Now that she's awake, that's when they're going to try and raise her." The silence grew thick with alarm, but Tara cut through it. "They're down in that cave with her. Fionn and I have been in there. There's plenty of room to hide. You can get lost in there *easily*."

"Yes," said Alva and Niall quietly, and Fionn remembered they once had a brother called Albert, who had met such a fate many years ago.

"The solstice is in two days' time!" said Elizabeth, pointing accusingly at Fionn. "If the Soulstalkers are really planning some kind of terrible coup, as you say, then why on *earth* haven't you done something about it?"

Fionn felt the question fill the room like a big dark cloud, crackling and swelling around them until sweat beaded on the back of his neck. He looked at his grandfather imploringly, but there was no answer shining in his eyes. There was only the truth now, and someone was going to have to say it.

"Well?" prompted Elizabeth.

With his gaze firmly pinned to the floorboards, Fionn took a deep breath and said, "My magic isn't working . . . It's never worked."

Elizabeth gasped.

"*What?*" spluttered Douglas.

"But you're the Storm Keeper!" cried Juliana. "You're supposed to be our guardian!"

"I know," said Fionn awkwardly. "But I can't wield the elements. They don't . . . well, they don't listen to me."

"*Yet*," said his grandfather.

Alva pressed a hand to her throat. "Oh, Fionn."

"Magic's not exactly *easy*," said Sam, rushing to Fionn's defense. "Being the Storm Keeper is a lot of pressure."

"It's only a matter of time before his magic kicks in," added Fionn's mother.

Elizabeth rounded on her. "Time we don't have!"

"We'll all be dead by the time he figures himself out," Douglas said, reeling. "Along with our animals!"

"Calm yourself," warned Niall. "This is hardly the lad's fault."

Juliana's hands were shaking so badly, she had to tuck them under her knees. "Well, what are we supposed to do if we don't have a proper Storm Keeper?"

"Isn't it obvious?" said Tara, with so much confidence the entire room turned to stare at her. "We defend ourselves. Those stupid Soulstalkers will be no match for an entire island!"

She grinned, her gaze shifting to the candle-lined shelves behind their shoulders.

Fionn shifted uncomfortably.

But before Tara could continue, Douglas pushed off the windowsill and began pacing the room, like a police detective. "What do we know about Morrigan and her followers?" he demanded. "What exactly are we dealing with here?" He peered down at Sam's dad, his mustache twitching expectantly. "Come on, Patton. You're the resident bard. You must know a thing or two about the old world?"

Mr. Patton closed his eyes and frowned, and just when Fionn thought he might rebuff Douglas or fall asleep from his sudden stillness, he cleared his throat and said in a voice halfway between a song and a prayer, "Let me tell you a tale of the Raven Queen."

Elizabeth sighed. "Oh, Douglas. *Truly*."

Fionn's grandfather crossed his legs and leaned back against the wall, like he was going on a serene boat ride. "Ah, the poet's tale."

"Go on, Dad," said Sam encouragingly. "We're listening."

"They say Morrigan was born in a village trapped in an eternal winter," Mr. Patton began solemnly. He kept his eyes closed, while Elizabeth rolled hers so hard the irises disappeared. "A pale, sickly place that rarely saw the sun. It teetered on the banks of a crystal lake that turned the town back on itself, its reflection rippling in the mouths of silverfish. The trees were drenched in snow and black with ravens, and they screeched endlessly, from sunrise to nightfall."

"Why did I ask?" muttered Douglas. "Why did I even ask?"

"*Shhh*," said Tara.

"Morrigan was born with power unlike anything her village had ever seen," Mr. Patton went on, unfazed. "Even so, she was not considered worthy of wearing her father's crown. She was much smaller and weaker than her older brothers, so she grew up alone and neglected. But her power grew with her."

Fionn frowned. He had never stopped to wonder where Morrigan had come from, or even if she had once been young. He had never considered the idea that she had been born into a family with parents and siblings, just as he'd been.

"This is absolute fantasy," said Elizabeth to no one in particular. "We did not come here for a performance."

"Speak for yourself, Betty," said Tom. "My TV's been broken for over a month."

"Morrigan's father was the head of her village," Mr. Patton continued. "He was fearless. *Feared.* But he longed to increase his influence, to control those who dwelled far beyond his own territory. After years of searching, he finally came upon a ritual that could increase his power many times over, but Morrigan stole it for herself. The old tales say she murdered her father and used his blood sacrifice to complete the ritual. But by doing so, she turned her magic dark. Powerful as it was, it could only work for evil deeds.

"Oh my *gosh,*" said Juliana.

Mr. Patton nodded somberly, and Fionn got the sense that he was enjoying this a bit too much. "After that,

Morrigan moved her reign of terror across the continents, killing all the magic-born and amassing mortal followers as she went. She strung them to her by their souls, which she wore around her neck. She was strong, and so were they. She was quick and violent, and they became so too. When she first set foot in Ireland, her cape rippled with twenty thousand trapped souls—soldiers made solely for killing and conquering, who hung on her every command. They set a course for Dagda and, well, the rest, as they say, is history." He stroked his chin thoughtfully, before adding, "Or, in this case, I suppose it's actually 'present.' "

He snapped his eyes open then, shook the story from his shoulders like a cloak, and shrugged. "That's the best I can do, lads."

Alva blinked. "You need to work on your endings, Phil."

"At least he had one," said Elizabeth snidely. "I thought I'd be in my grave before he finished."

"I *wish*," muttered Fionn.

Sam chuckled.

"Well, we can all thank our wonderful Storm Keeper for welcoming these terrible creatures so readily to Arranmore," said Elizabeth. "The most obvious and dangerous invasion in recent history, and you couldn't lift a *finger* to stop it. Any worthy Storm Keeper could have toppled those boats with the flick of their wrist yesterday. Douglas says you were even out on the strand watching them when they moored! Truly, Fionn, your incompetence is *unparalleled*."

Fionn's mother threw her a withering look. "If I recall correctly, it was the Beasley family who first welcomed Ivan to these shores, who shared the secrets of the Storm Keeper with him and no doubt helped him find his way to Morrigan's grave in the first place."

"Yeah," said Tara, matching the intensity of their mother's glare. "If they're so *obvious* and *dangerous*, why were you cozying up to one all summer?"

"Well, Ivan was entirely different from those . . . those *zombies*," said Douglas, in a bluster. "He looked like one of us—talked that way too! The lad was smart and cunning and *manipulative*. He was persuasive in a way we could hardly *resist*. Perhaps it was a kind of magic. Who knows?"

"Or a kind of stupidity," muttered Tom Rowan. "The man was an oddball from the outset. He braided his *beard*, for Dagda's sake."

Fionn wondered at Douglas's words. He had been wrestling with the same thought all night—haunted by Ivan's face in his dreams. Why was Ivan so different from the other Soulstalkers? How had he been able to walk and talk like a normal human, to reel the Beasleys into his web of lies?

"Let's not dwell on insignificant details," said Elizabeth dismissively. "Here is what we have so astutely established during this seemingly endless hour. The Soulstalkers are here, and their numbers are increasing with every ferry that arrives. As yet, we have seen no sign of Ivan, but his ilk are affecting the health of the island and in two days, if the *rumor* is to be believed, they plan to raise Morrigan." Elizabeth settled her icy gaze on Fionn. "The question is, what does our disgraced Storm Keeper plan to do about it? Or do you intend to stand by and watch us die, one by one?"

"Without a shred of magic to defend ourselves," added Douglas sourly.

Fionn's mother cleared her throat pointedly. "Well, actually, that's not quite the case."

"We *do* have magic," said Tara.

There was a sharp intake of breath, the whole sitting room inhaling as one.

Douglas snapped his head up, and Elizabeth's eyes grew suddenly very wide.

Chapter Eight

THE TEMPORARY TORNADO

Tara plucked a candle from the shelf, and Fionn leaped to his feet without meaning to. "The Soulstalkers are nowhere near as strong as they used to be," he said quickly. "I spoke with Lír yesterday, in another layer, and she told me that they're weak without their leader. They don't have their true strength. At least not while Morrigan is still buried. They're only shells really, half alive and half dead."

Elizabeth threw up her hands. "Oh, so the Queen of the merrows has weighed in, has she? Nice of Lír to give us her two cents. I don't suppose she'd bother to help with this mess, would she? Or are you so ineffective that you forgot to ask her, in whatever layer you were wandering around in?"

"Actually, the merrows *can* help us," said Fionn, ignoring Tara's prickly glare. "In fact, that's my whole idea."

"*Fionn*," said his mother. "That is not the idea we're here to discuss."

Fionn ignored her. The magic of the Storm Keeper's candles was hardly a secret—for centuries they had carried islanders to different layers, stored thunderstorms and heat-waves and everything in between. But their second use—as weapons with magic to control the elements—was not widely known. The idea of imminently revealing a roomful of powerful weapons to two very hostile Beasleys, not to mention a bunch of people who wouldn't have the first clue what to do with them, seemed like madness to Fionn. Especially when they hadn't even discussed the possibility of finding the Tide Summoner.

He went on determinedly. "All we have to do is find the shell that binds the merrows to the island. It's big and white and sparkly, and it's called the Tide Summoner, and it's somewhere on the island. Hughie Rua had it last, so it might be around the area where he used to live, or even in someone's attic or shed! Once we find it, we can summon the merrows to destroy these invaders once and for all, and keep the rest of them from ever darkening our shores—"

"Fionn!" hissed Tara. "What are you *doing*?"

Fionn blinked the room back into focus, only to find

the islanders staring at him with varying degrees of incredulity.

"You want us to go and look for a . . . shell?" said Alva delicately.

"Like, a *sea*shell?" clarified Juliana.

"*That's* the grand plan?" said Douglas.

Elizabeth rolled her eyes. "Dagda save us all."

Niall *hmm*'d under his breath, a muscle working in his jaw as he stared at Fionn.

"Stop talking about the stupid shell," said Tara frustratedly. "We've already discussed this. We need to tell them about the candles. About what they can *really* do."

Elizabeth turned her attention to Tara. "Go on," she said, intrigued.

Fionn whirled around, looking helplessly at his grandfather.

"It's all right, lad," he said gently. "Let her show them."

That was enough permission for Tara. She plucked a candle from the shelf, Fionn's mother handing her a lighter at the same time. "Nothing too showy," she warned. "Or we'll have a big cleanup on our hands."

Tara blinked slowly, as though savoring the moment. Then she marched into the middle of the sitting room, stepping over Sam as she ripped the anchor from the bottom of the candle.

Juliana gasped, then promptly covered her mouth. "Sorry. I thought something was going to happen."

"It is," said Fionn's mother with a smile. "Watch."

Tara flicked her lighter and brought it to the bottom of the wick. The islanders bent forward in their seats to watch the flame crawl up inside the wax. The second it disappeared, Tara curled her fist around it.

"This candle holds a limited supply of the Storm Keeper's magic," said Fionn's mother. "For the time it takes for the wax to burn, the wielder can control the elements in their environment."

Tara stuck her hand out in front of her. "Earth, air, water, fire. All it takes is a little concentration."

Suddenly the cottage windows flew open and the wind rushed in. It flapped in the end of Tara's hoodie and lifted the hair from her head, until it looked like she was standing in the dead center of a hurricane. This time, everyone gasped. Fionn didn't miss the way Elizabeth glanced at Douglas, her eyes growing big and greedy.

"Every one of Dagda's descendants can be taught, if they're willing to learn," said Fionn's mother.

Tara flicked her wrist and the couch was swept backward by a wall of wind, taking Alva, Juliana, Niall, and Tom along with it.

Juliana shrieked, and Tom laughed, the islanders'

surprise turning to giddy excitement as Tara rolled her hand in a circle, swirling the gust into a thin tornado. She sent it skipping around the room, giggling as Sam sprang up to run from it, only to trip over his father's feet and land on top of Fionn's grandfather. Elizabeth reached out to touch it, yelping as her hand was blown backward, nearly slapping her in the face. Douglas covered his head as it danced around him, and Sam's dad simply shook his head in delighted disbelief.

And then it was over—the candle lay crushed inside Tara's fist, and the wind scattered to the far corners of the island, slamming the windows shut on its way out. She dropped her hand and flexed her fingers. "*Voilà*."

Fionn's grandfather chuckled. "Well done, Tara. Excellent work."

The rest of the room sat in stunned silence.

Even the Beasleys were speechless, and Fionn, despite his squirming jealousy, felt the barest flicker of smugness at the look on Elizabeth's face.

"Well," said Niall, easily tugging the couch back to its rightful place despite the three other people currently sitting on it. "That was impressive."

"Impressive is an understatement," said Alva. "When do we get to try?"

"This afternoon." Tara was grinning so wide, Fionn

could barely look at her. "We have thousands of candles. I'm going to bring some to the school hall later and hold a training session with anyone who wants to learn. It's really easy," she said, lazily peeling strips of wax from her fingers. "It won't take much practice."

"Count us in," said Alva.

"We'll rally the troops," said Sam's dad.

Fionn's mother curled a hand on Tara's shoulder, her eyes shining with the success of a plan coming together. Their plan.

Fionn's grandfather smiled encouragingly at him, but Fionn could see the pity in his expression, so he looked away, feeling sour, despite the success of Tara's demonstration. He was supposed to lead the island, and here he was, curled up by the fireplace, failing to lead their own meeting.

"Go back and spread word to the other islanders," said Fionn's mother. "Tell anyone who doesn't want to be a part of the coming conflict to leave as soon as they can. Any descendants interested in wielding the Storm Keeper's magic should meet us in the school hall at three this afternoon. Non-descendants are welcome to come along, but they won't actually be able to use the candles," she said, smiling at Juliana, who looked at once jealous and relieved.

And then all at once the sun was high, and the cookies were gone, and everyone was clambering back into their coats and scarves and gloves and hats, until their chins disappeared, and then their noses too, as they were sent out into the frigid morning air with renewed purpose and whipped down the headland by an icy gust.

Niall lingered a moment in the doorway. "I think I heard a story once about that shell you mentioned," he said to Fionn in a low voice. "It was an old favorite of Patrick the Story Weaver's. He was a Cannon Storm Keeper."

Fionn felt himself swell with anticipation. "Yeah," he said eagerly. "I've heard of him. He founded the library."

Niall nodded. "There were rumors of a seashell that could call the merrows home. I used to search the beaches for it as a boy, when I wasn't out looking for Aonbharr." He smiled to himself. "If Hughie Rua really was the last to see it, you could try searching the old Freedom house."

"Freedom house?" said Fionn, with confusion.

"The McCauley farmhouse," said Niall, wrapping his scarf over his mouth so that his words were muffled. "I suppose it's more of a ruin now. It's the one Hughie Rua built when he was alive." He pointed vaguely in the direction of east. "Your mom knows it. Her parents left the land to her in their will—not that you can grow anything there these days."

"Oh." Fionn nodded in delayed understanding. "Yeah, I know that place. I just didn't realize it had a name."

Niall shrugged. "Everything here has a name. Hughie named it after his boat. *Saoirse*. Means 'freedom.' "

Fionn frowned. Something was stirring in the back of his mind, a thought flitting by, too quick to catch. "H*mm*."

"Well, he *was* the great protector of our freedom, after all," said Niall with a wink. "Storm Keepers and their egos. Not you though, Fionn. The Boyles have always been responsible with the role. You were right to ask us for help today. We'll handle this together." He waved as he stalked down the garden path. "See you later."

The Beasleys were the last to leave, Elizabeth insisting on using the bathroom and then loudly complaining about the brand of hand soap to Douglas as they finally left the cottage. "It gives me hives, Douglas. It's that awful *cheap* formula . . ."

Not thirty seconds after Fionn had shut the door behind them, his mother came out, waving Elizabeth's dead-badger hat. "She left this on the sink, Fionn. Will you run after her before she gets home and accuses us of stealing it?"

Fionn groaned his way outside, took the hat into the wind, and fleetingly considered flinging it over the cliffs and into the sea below.

Elizabeth turned around long before he reached her, her hand outstretched, as though she had been expecting him. "Oh, how clumsy of me, Fionn. And that hat was *so* expensive."

"You should have just asked Tom to shoot one for you." Fionn stuffed it into her hand and turned on his heel.

"Run along home, Storm Keeper!" she called after him. "Let the adults handle this little mess you've made."

Fionn glared at her over his shoulder. "We're all handling it *together*."

"It's not really a group task, though, is it, Fionn? The guardianship of this place." Her smile was a perfect pale crescent. "But then, every Storm Keeper is different. There are some that bring great honor to their family name and then, well, there are some that bring shame." She sighed dramatically. "I suppose, as islanders, we can't *all* take after Hughie Rua . . ." Fionn could sense it before she said it, the dark arrow hovering on her tongue. "Some of us are destined to end up like Cormac Boyle." She opened her mouth and shot it at him. "Utterly *forgotten*."

It landed in the center of Fionn's heart, and he felt, for a second, like he might crumple. "*Get lost*, Betty."

He marched up the headland so fast, he didn't feel the searing cold—only the heat of his rage as it razed a trail through his body. The wind came with him, howling just as angrily. When he got home, the door slammed so hard, the hinges rattled. A hat leaped off the coatrack and flew across the room, where it hit the wall and tumbled to the floor.

His grandfather shot up from his chair by the fireplace. "Whoa, whoa, whoa! What did my favorite hat ever do to you?"

"I didn't even touch it," said Fionn. "It did that on its own."

"I know," said his grandfather, eyeing it uneasily.

Fionn plucked the hat off the floor and stalked back to the coatrack, where he hung it back up, before shrugging his coat on.

"Where are you off to now?" asked his grandfather.

"To do something useful," said Fionn, swinging the door open. He was outside and into the wind before his grandfather could answer him.

Chapter Nine

THE FREEDOM MEMORY

While Tara spent the rest of the day in the school hall, training willing islanders in the secret art of candle magic, Fionn scoured the ruins of the old McCauley farmhouse. Sam joined him in his efforts, stoically surrendering the chance to attend the magic lesson in order to pursue the legend of the Tide Summoner with his best friend. An afternoon of fruitless searching gave way to an evening of the same, Fionn and Sam crawling around in the frost-slick grass, while the ghost of Fionn's McCauley ancestry yielded nothing but numb fingers and wet socks.

When night fell, they trudged home along the strand, greeted by reports of the evening ferries, which had brought two hundred more blank faces across the narrow slip of sea. Another regiment marched inland and then disappeared down the craggy underside of the island.

After a late dinner of his grandfather's beef-and-Guinness stew, Fionn lay awake scanning the shelves in the darkness. He noted the missing candles, since sacrificed to his sister's lessons. She had taken the bare minimum, but Fionn still worried over the loss. Tomorrow, more magic would be donated in aid of island practice, creating new gaps that would remind him of all the ways he was failing his people. How the islanders who had once respected him now looked at him with a mixture of pity and betrayal. How they had turned to his own sister for leadership.

And why wouldn't they? They knew his secret, after all.

Magic Barren.

Useless.

The wind howled outside the little cottage on the headland, pressed its hands against the windows, and shook them in their frames, as if the island was trying to tell him something.

The bond that takes a touch to make

Will not before a lifetime break.

But the bond *had* been broken. Hughie Rua was long dead. So where did he leave the Tide Summoner?

Lay worthy hands upon the shell,

And breath becomes the ocean's knell.

Fionn studied his hands in the dark. Were they even worthy of the Tide Summoner? He turned over on the couch, pulled the blanket up around his ears. When he finally fell asleep, he dreamed of the mainland. He glimpsed rolling green hills and newly paved streets, little towns made from cobblestones and colored flags. He recognized the different patterns, each county a notch in Ireland's curved spine.

Fionn saw Ivan standing beneath the Dublin spire, the column rising like a sharp tooth in the darkness. Morrigan's laugh rushed through him. She was gleeful, expectant.

Tick-tock, Storm Keeper.

Tick-tock, comes the Reaper.

Fionn felt his skin peel away, his bones plucked from his skeleton and stacked one by one, until they made a spire as tall and white as the one in his mind.

Dublin.

Ivan was in Dublin.

The clock was getting louder.

It set the tempo of his pulse.

Tick-tock, tick-tock, tick-TOCK, TICK-TOCK, TICK-TOCK—

He woke, gasping. Fionn felt as if he had swallowed a ball of fire, and it was torching him from the inside out. His fingertips were crackling. He curled them into fists and breathed through his nose, to keep from vomiting all over himself.

A shard of moonlight slipped through the window and crept all the way up to the couch. Fionn looked around, making his eyes as wide as he could in the darkness. The shelf in the corner was shaking.

There was a thought prodding at him.

Think, said a voice in his head. *Remember.*

He wandered over to the shelf. The moonlight came with him, dusting itself along the labels as Fionn's magic glowed like an ember in his chest.

The thought was crystallizing. It was a memory, and it came in Niall Cannon's voice. *Hughie named it after his boat.* Saoirse. *Means "freedom."*

Fionn stared at the candles.

Well, he was *the great protector of our freedom, after all.*

Seven blizzards in a row. A handful of summer skies. Autumn showers and winter winds. *Sean McCauley's Runaway Kite*... Storms and storms and storms and storms. *Unexpected Tornado at Josie's Twelfth Birthday Party.* Ribbon lightning, sheet lightning, forked lightning, flash lightning... *Hurricane Ophelia.* Snow days and snowstorms. Sunsets and sunrises. *Suaimhneas*, which meant "peace," and *Saoirse*, which meant—

Fionn froze.

Saoirse.

Freedom.

Was it possible?

Had it been here all this time, sitting right under his nose?

He reached out to take the candle, and a breeze curled around it like a finger. It knocked it from the shelf.

Fionn caught it in midair. "I was about to do that," he said aloud.

The candle was tall and thin, like a stick of dynamite, the wax as inky as a pirate's sail. Fionn dipped his nose in and almost sneezed. *Gunpowder*—the thickness of it rested along the top like froth on a cappuccino. Then came the rest: a violent storm flung from an angry horizon, capillaries of lightning burning fissures in the sky. Shattered wood and burning flags, ash and fire, and cast-iron cannonballs soaring through an open sea. Blood and bone and seaweed, all tangled up in the salt-filled gurgle of drowning men.

Fionn bristled as the dredges of *Saoirse* crawled up his nose—crusted barnacles and scales the color of burned silver, a shark's grin bearing down on human skin.

Merrows.

He stared at the candle.

All this time, Hughie Rua had been living in *Tír na nÓg.*

And the Tide Summoner along with him.

Fionn didn't know if it was funny or maddening, but he laughed anyway. The sound hung in the air like a melody and sung him to sleep with the candle tight in his fist.

This time, when he closed his eyes, he dreamed of adventure.

Chapter Ten

THE THIRD MUSKETEER

When Fionn awoke early the following morning, there was a clock ticking in the back of his mind. The countdown to the winter solstice had dwindled to one final day, but he felt emboldened by his late-night discovery. He uncurled his fist and smiled at the candle.

The Tide Summoner was within his grasp.

In the kitchen, someone had left a wicker basket on the table. Fionn was used to deliveries like this turning up every so often, either deposited on the doorstep or, if it was raining, left inside the door. He thought they might have stopped coming once his mother arrived during the summer, but they only grew larger, and none of them, his mother included, ever complained about it.

He rolled off the couch and wandered into the kitchen to inspect it. There were fresh eggs and orange juice with pulp, a loaf of brown bread and a carton of milk. There were carrots and parsnips and an uncooked chicken. A packet of sliced ham. A block of orange cheese. A jar of French mustard—the expensive kind. A family-size chocolate bar. A big box of tea bags and two packs of cookies—gingersnaps and custard creams. There was a note hanging off the side:

A few extras this week. —Rose.

"Rose," he said, out loud.

Rose. Of course.

His phone buzzed, startling him.

It was a text from Sam.

There in 15. And believe I'm bringing SNACKS ☺

Sam was waiting for Fionn down on the beach, skimming stones along the waves. Fionn jogged to meet him, his grin so wide it vibrated in his cheeks. By the end of the day, they would have the Tide Summoner in hand and an army of merrows to command. The Soulstalkers wouldn't live to see the solstice. This one, or any more to come. Elizabeth Beasley would see what bravery looked like then, how good a Storm Keeper he could really be. He was going to save the island before it fell to ruin. He was going to make his family proud of him. He was going to make *himself* proud. "Are you ready for a pirate adventure?"

Sam yanked his scarf down. "I've been waiting my whole life for a pirate adventure. Of course I'm—" His face fell as he caught sight of something over Fionn's shoulder. "Oh *no*."

Fionn heard her before he saw her, her sneakers thumping across the damp sand, her laughter floating through the air. "Fiooooooonn!"

Fionn whirled around just in time to catch Shelby Beasley as she flung herself at him. She squeezed the last morsel of air from his lungs, her hair streaming into his face and his mouth and his eyes until everything was the color of sand. She pulled away, her braces winking at him when she said, "Hello, stranger! Miss me?"

"Of course!" Fionn couldn't contain his happiness. The day had already brought untold possibility, and now that his friend had returned from the mainland, a pocketful of adventure awaited the three of them. "I thought you weren't coming for Christmas!"

"We weren't going to, but then my uncle called my dad in a fit yesterday even though my granny told him not to, and after a lot of panic about a bunch of Soulstalkers and a looming solstice from Doug, and some definite emotional spiraling from my dad, my mom decided we should all come and use our wits to help you stave off encroaching oblivion!" She grinned at him. "So . . . *surprise!* My present is my presence. Have I missed anything else?"

The reunion was hurried, peppered with brief talk of the island's growing population of Soulstalkers, the possibility of Morrigan returning, Fionn's nonexistent magic, and Tara's new starring role as the island's champion. Talk turned then to the Tide Summoner and the merrows that had been bonded to it—an army they all agreed was far better equipped to face an ancient, gathering evil than one that relied on the very mortal members of their own families and a bevy of candles that were in limited supply.

Mercifully, the Tide Summoner was closer than ever and, now armed with the freedom candle, Fionn was determined to take back control—to prove himself once and for all, and save the island without endangering its people.

As the conversation turned to the present day, and the task at hand opened before them like a storybook, one among them seemed suddenly and utterly unenthused.

"Why are you scowling?" Fionn asked Sam, when they had finished going over the particulars.

Shelby turned on him. "You've just found your third musketeer!"

"I didn't make enough sandwiches," said Sam sourly.

Fionn waved his concern away. "That's all right. I'm not that hungry anyway."

"Well, you should have told me that." Sam folded his arms and pushed his bottom lip out. "I made three different varieties, and everything."

"I thought you said you didn't make enough," said Fionn, bewildered.

Sam glanced sidelong at Shelby. "I meant I didn't make enough for *her*."

Shelby narrowed her eyes at Sam. "Are you *jealous*?"

Sam scoffed unconvincingly. "Why on earth would I be jealous of *you*, a near-stranger appearing out of nowhere and crashing *my* adventure with *my* best friend?" He looked at Fionn, his eyebrows raised. "Don't you think we should take a vote on this?"

Shelby pulled her hat down, tucking her hair behind her ears. "You're right. We *should* vote. Fionn? Do you think we should let Sam come on our adventure?"

Sam's eyes went wide. "You just got here! It's *our* adventure!"

"But I was here first," Shelby returned with practiced nonchalance. "So, I get first dibs. *Dibs!*"

Sam rounded on her. "You can't be serious!"

Shelby cackled wickedly. "Oh, lighten up, Patton.

You'll warm to me soon enough. I'll grow on you." She beamed at him. "Like a rash."

Sam looked at Fionn imploringly. "She's a *Beasley*," he mouthed.

"I can see what you're saying," said Shelby. "I'm standing right in front of you."

"She's fine," said Fionn to Sam. "She's really brave."

"So am I," said Sam petulantly.

"I didn't say you weren't brave," said Fionn.

"You're probably not as brave as me, though," interjected Shelby. "I once tried to tackle a meerkat at Dublin Zoo."

Sam stared at her. "How is that relevant?"

Fionn sighed.

"Because I'm not afraid of anything," Shelby emphasized.

"Meerkats are tiny," said Sam.

"Not when you're *three* they're not!"

"Well, last year, in London, I fought a mugger off with my flute," said Sam. "A flute that once belonged to my great-grandmother, Maggie Patton, by the way."

"If you're so brave, where were you last summer when Fionn almost *died* in that cave?"

"I was actually in Port Antonio visiting my nan," said Sam. "She lives halfway across the world on the island of Jamaica. There are moths as big as dinner plates there, and hummingbirds as small as eggs, and I'm not scared of *either*!"

"Why would you be afraid of a hummingbird?" scoffed Shelby. "While you were off playing Disney princesses with friendly birds, *we* were stuck over here getting beaten up by a storm!"

Fionn groaned. "Can you two give it a rest, please? The world is big and scary in lots of different ways, and you're both *incredibly* brave, but we still do have a Soulstalker situation to worry about, you know."

"Look. I haven't had a *proper* best friend since I moved back to this place," said Sam, kicking sand up onto his shoes. "And we've got a good thing going here."

"News flash—you can have more than one best friend," said Shelby.

"No, you can't," said Sam, shaking his head. "Not while the world is ending."

"Oh, don't be such a pessimist," said Shelby. "If you're going to be all doom and gloom, you should just stay at home and write poetry."

"Hey, my dad's a poet and he's perfectly happy!" Sam glared at her. "And at least he doesn't go around giving people new faces for no reason."

"My mom is a *cardiac* surgeon," said Shelby pointedly.

"And before you start on my dad, corporate accounting is the backbone of this country."

Fionn pinched the bridge of his nose. "Can we all just be friends? We're running low on time and I think if you two got to know each other, you'd get along like a house on fire."

"What is it exactly about a burning house that says *good vibes* to you?" said Sam.

Shelby tried to trap her laugh but it seeped out through her fingers. "Oh *no*," she muttered.

There was a long silence, Shelby and Sam looking each other up and down, like adversaries in a boxing ring, until finally Shelby broke. "I like your coat," she said grudgingly.

"Thanks," said Sam a little stiffly. "It's peacock blue. Very hard to get. I like your shoes. The sparkles are cool."

"I glued them on myself," said Shelby.

"Cool," said Sam, relenting.

"Thanks," said Shelby.

And with that, the iceberg between them thawed just enough to see over it. The planning resumed in earnest. There were logistics to consider—three people and one candle among the most pertinent of concerns. The solution was a tenuous one, but after much deliberation over three free hot chocolates from Donal's shop, coupled with the entire contents of Sam's sandwich bag, the last remnants of Sonia Patton's banana bread, and a packet of mints donated by Shelby, they decided what to do.

After a detour to the lifeboat station, they traipsed back up the headland with three orange life jackets and enough rope to moor a cruise ship. They convened outside *Tír na nÓg*, where the sun squatted like a brass coin in a pale sky.

"You sure this will work?" Sam asked Shelby as she looped the blue rope beneath his life jacket, knotting it expertly, before threading it through the other side.

"I mean, the *rope* will hold. My gran taught me all sorts of sailor's knots when I was small," said Shelby, her fingers nimble as she worked. "But I have no idea if it will *work* work . . ."

Fionn slipped his own life jacket over his head, pulling the straps tight. "I think it will, since we're all connected. The wind won't be able to separate us."

Shelby wound the rope around Fionn's waist, creating the same intricate knot. Finally, she tied herself in. "There," she said, dusting her hands. "All done."

Fionn removed the candle from his pocket and handed it to her. "Great. Let's get going."

Shelby's fingers hovered over the candle. "What? Me?"

"I can't hold it in case I'm seen," Fionn reminded her.

"There are way too many people in this memory. And besides, I need to be free to grab the Tide Summoner."

"Oh, okay. Right." Shelby closed her fingers around the candle. "So, I just light it?"

"I thought you were brave," said Sam.

"I *am* brave," she said quickly. "The rope just chafed my hands, and I'm not sure if I can grip the lighter properly. It's just . . . Oh, I don't know." She handed the candle to him, looking at her shoes when she added, "You should do it. You're Maggie Patton's great-grandson, after all."

Sam took the candle. "You make an excellent point. I suppose I'll rise to the occasion and lead us into our perilous adventure."

The cottage door shut with a bang, and from the garden of *Tír na nÓg* came a noise like a shrieking goat. Bartley Beasley was halfway down the path, doubled over on himself with laughter. Tara was standing beside him.

"*Fionn*," she said, her hand flying to her mouth. "What on earth are you three doing?"

"Ehh . . . ," said Fionn.

Shelby looked around her. "Umm . . ."

"Well . . . ," said Sam. "This is awkward."

Bartley wiped the tears from his eyes, his pinched mouth straining against his cheeks. Defying all possible odds, his hair was even *higher* than the last time Fionn had seen him. It must have been at least four inches now, the tip of it swaying back and forth in the breeze. Of course, he wasn't wearing a hat, his ridiculous hairdo adding to his already obnoxious personality. "Shel, look at the state of you." He took out his phone and snapped a photo. "I'm definitely putting this online!"

Tara placed a hand on Bartley's arm. "Don't," she said in a low voice. "They're our siblings. It's embarrassing for all of us."

How Tara had managed to forgive Bartley for stranding her in that Sea Cave remained a mystery to Fionn. They had gone down the steps together, and at the first sign of danger, Bartley had swum away and saved himself, leaving Tara at the mercy of the Sea Cave's sinister current. If Fionn hadn't found his way to her inside those dark tunnels, she might not have made it back at all. He could hardly stand to think about it.

It was like his mother always said: *Rose-colored glasses disguise red flags*—and Bartley was draped in them. Fionn was all for second chances, but only for people who *deserved* them. It was quite clear to anyone with half a brain that Bartley was wholly and eternally irredeemable.

"What is this crap?" said Bartley, striding out to assess them at close range. "Are you going swimming or drowning?" He picked at the rope. "Shel, can't you do better than these morons? Come down to the school hall with us instead. Tara's going to teach me how to use the candles." He smirked at Fionn. "You needed a leader, Boyle? Well, here I am. And just in time too, by the sound of it."

"Fionn's the Storm Keeper, Bartley," said Shelby, her finger raised in warning. "You have to show him some respect."

Bartley snorted. "He can have my respect when he earns it. Do I look scared of him?"

"No," interjected Sam. "But you do look jealous."

Bartley rounded on him. "What would I possibly be jealous about, Patton?"

"Well, clearly, we're about to go on a very important mission," said Sam coolly. "One that you are not invited on."

Fionn grinned at Tara. "Tell Mom and Grandad that I know where the Tide Summoner is, and I'm going to go and bring it back!"

Tara blinked at him. "Are you seriously still chasing that old shell?"

"You mean the shell that's going to save our island?" said Fionn pointedly. "Yeah, I am."

This time, Bartley opened his mouth to respond, but Sam interrupted him. "Sorry, Baz. You'd just stink up the journey with your poor attitude and ridiculous hairdo." He jabbed the candle at Shelby, who flicked the lighter open in one fell swoop.

In the blink of an eye, the three of them were catapulted away from their layer of Arranmore and into a different one entirely, leaving Bartley Beasley gaping after them like a slack-jawed fish.

Chapter Eleven

THE GRINNING PIRATE

The rope curled and straightened, whipping the air, like it was trying to break itself. They held on tight to it, their palms chafing as the wind tried to cleave them apart. The island seemed to give up then, squishing them back together and scooping them into its busy hands.

"It's working!" shouted Sam.

Shelby's laughter pealed into the sky. "I can't believe it!"

The land morphed around them. The seasons blinked from winter to summer, summer to autumn, while the sun and moon flipped back and forth like a pancake. The months turned to years and the years turned to decades as the 1700s hurtled toward them with impossible speed.

They were pushed up and around the rim of the headland, to where the land turned jagged and uneven, and dark cliffs climbed high above stony beaches. Sam waved the candle back and forth, the flame devouring what little heat was left in the air as they were spun into an ice-cold winter morning that shook the island by its edges. They were released in the lap of a low-sloping cliff.

Overhead, the first rays of sunrise brushed the sky with amber and pink.

They clambered over craggy rocks and slimy seaweed, carefully picking their way down to the cove below, where the strand was slim and curving, like a crescent moon.

Fionn had never been to this beach before but there was something eerily familiar about it.

Then he remembered what it was, and the realization stopped him in his tracks. "We're close to Morrigan's Sea Cave," he said, teetering on the edge of a rock. "The entrance is just beyond this cove."

Sam clapped a steadying hand on his shoulder. "It's 1728, mate. She's fast asleep."

"Right. Yeah." Fionn's shoulders loosened, and slowly, carefully, he resumed his descent.

By the time they reached the cove, an old storm was snarling at them from the horizon. A ring of purple clouds lumbered across the sea, hovering above three colossal rocks that speared from the ocean like carving knives.

"Whoa," said Fionn, craning his neck.

"Black Point Rock," said Shelby. "Haven't you seen the sea stacks up close before?"

Fionn shook his head. "They're so much bigger than I thought."

"My dad tried to climb them when he was a teenager and got caught on one of its spires," said Shelby, sliding down onto the sand and adding "Sorry, sorry, sorry" as she pulled the others with her by the rope. "He broke three bones in his leg. It was Malachy who brought him back to shore. Used the wind to carry him over the sea."

"He really should have known better," said Sam. "My dad says Black Point Rock is cursed."

Shelby shrugged. "Dad and Uncle Doug were always doing stupid stuff like that."

"Is *everything* here cursed?" asked Fionn.

"Miracles and curses. That's the currency of Arranmore." Sam blew out a breath, his gaze pulled skyward to where the sheer cliffs now peered over them. "There's a woman standing over on that cliff."

They looked up, frowning. There was indeed an old woman standing on the edge of the headland. She was bent almost to the ground, a gray shawl wrapped around her head and shoulders.

"I thought nobody on the island knew about the pirate invasion until it was over," said Shelby. "Didn't Hughie sneak out when everyone was asleep?"

"Well, clearly not everyone," said Sam. "It almost seems like she's looking at *us* . . ."

"That's impossible." For a heartbeat, Fionn thought he recognized her—but the idea of it was absurd. They were in 1728, and old women like Rose were hardly a new invention of Arranmore. He was only thinking of her now because of the food basket this morning.

"She's not watching us, she's watching *him*. Look!" Shelby pointed to the shallows, where a wooden sailing boat was gliding out to sea, its maroon sails stretched taut in the gathering wind. On the starboard side of the hull, in looping white paint, was the word *Saoirse*. Out in front, with one foot propped up on the bow, stood a towering beast of a man. His legs were the size of tree trunks; his burly arms were pale as moonlight; and his long hair was the exact shade of a mandarin orange. It whipped out behind him, dancing on the swelling winds as he bared his face to the open sea.

Fionn's magic blinked an eye open, and he laughed without meaning to. He had seen this same Storm Keeper in Cowan's Lake, and now here he stood, made of flesh and bone. "Hughie Rua! That's him!"

"He looks just like he did in the lake!" said Sam gleefully.

"Do you see the Tide Summoner anywhere?" asked Shelby, standing on her tiptoes.

"No." Fionn was doing the very same thing.

"I think we'll have to follow him out," said Sam.

Fionn pressed a hand to his chest to calm the sudden rush of nerves. He remembered his life jacket, coarse under his fingers and puffed up to his chin. He might be going out to sea again, but at least he would float if he had to.

Be brave, he told himself. *Be like Hughie.*

At the end of the cove, two small rowboats had been moored to the cliffside. They unknotted the larger of the two and dragged it across the sand. They pushed it out into the current, clambering into it one after the other, while the blue rope strained between them.

The storm picked up.

The sky darkened.

Fionn and Shelby grabbed an oar each, and Sam held the candle high, as the memory hitched their course to Hughie Rua's. Their little boat was welcomed by the current and pulled into the unseen shadows of the *Saoirse*.

In the distance, a whip of lightning fissured the sky in two, heralding the arrival of three pirate ships with billowing black sails. They skulked through the low-hanging clouds like crocodiles.

Hughie Rua adjusted his own sails, until the *Saoirse* was traveling at an alarming rate. He threw his arms out wide, gathering the tide and pulling it under him. The sailboat rose up ten feet, then twenty, climbing the mound of the ocean until he was riding on his own tidal wave.

The unseen adventurers cried out as the wind reached down and dragged them up after it. The world tilted suddenly. Their rowboat was almost vertical, the water sloshing them from side to side as they lay back against each other, grabbing hands and arms and legs and feet.

"We're climbing the sea!" shouted Sam, a fistful of froth exploding in his face.

"I feel like we're going up a roller coaster!" said Shelby, the ends of her damp hair splayed out like eels along Fionn's chest.

"Hold on!" yelled Fionn, sounding much braver than he felt. "Watch that candle, Sam!"

They climbed over the hump of the wave, the bow dropping as they drew level with the cliff tops. The old woman was still there, hunched like an ancient statue.

Hughie's sailboat was just three lengths ahead, hovering above the roiling ocean.

The enemy fleet quickened its advance, their sharp-nosed hulls puncturing the storm clouds. The decks were crowded with pirates; some of them were swinging from hanging nets, long guns slung over their shoulders as they tried to climb closer to the *Saoirse*.

"They must have a death wish," said Sam, peering down on them.

"They'll be trounced!" said Shelby giddily.

Fionn tried to swallow his nerves. There was an eerie familiarity creeping over him. Though the ships were larger and more intricate than the ancient vessels that had first brought Morrigan to Arranmore, there was something about those black sails . . . the speed with which they were plowing through the ocean . . .

The memory quickened and the thought evaporated. The sea climbed again and they climbed with it, perched precariously on Hughie Rua's magical wave, with the world looking up at them. The clouds wreathed their shoulders, static crackling along their skin and plucking strands of hair from under their hats.

There was a ship directly below them now.

Fionn squinted at the letters scrawled along its hull, pressed the name between his lips: *The Corpus*.

The wave started to bubble.

"Why do I suddenly feel like we're about to die?" shouted Sam.

Shelby groaned. "I wish we hadn't eaten all those sandwiches!"

Fionn gripped the sides of the boat. Up ahead, his ancestor crouched down and threaded one arm through the anchor chain.

The candle in Sam's fist was shaking violently. "I regret this decision," he called over his shoulder, just as Hughie released a triumphant shout, pulled his free hand into his chest, and closed it into a fist.

The sky ignited. There were three awful seconds of nothingness when both vessels seemed to hang by an invisible thread, then the wind snapped and the sky roared and the world dropped.

The wave surged over *The Corpus*, taking them all with it, screaming at the top of their lungs. Hughie Rua threw his head back and laughed as they flew down, down, down, following his billowing sails into the sea. The wind pulled their cheeks from their mouths and stole their breath, their stomachs flipping upside down and inside out as they cut through the air.

Their screams ran their voices hoarse before they hit the water.

Then they left the world behind them, piercing the skin of the ocean in two identical points.

In the murky blue-blackness, Shelby's hand found Fionn's, and Fionn's hand found Sam's. Their life jackets swelled around their necks, their rope stretched taut between them as the current tried to tear them apart. The ocean flung them out, and they found themselves bobbing on a changing tide without a boat beneath them. Sam waved the sopping candle at Fionn. The sea had extinguished it.

With their breath shuddering from them in staccato gulps, and the wheels of time spinning them, Fionn grabbed the candle from Sam and pressed his lighter to the wick.

A flame sprang up instantly, and the wind cut into Fionn.

They caught the memory by its tail, and Fionn was turned to flesh inside it. The sea hiccuped, and from below, the rowboat slammed into them, bruising the backs of their legs as it lifted them out of the water. They were flung forward, their oars spinning furiously, as they glided into a mess of black sails and broken masts. The tidal wave had drowned *The Corpus*. Now it was floating as driftwood along the waves, the desperate cries of dying pirates making bubbles in the froth.

Fionn reached for the edge of a sail, the hem sodden between his fingers. From the deep, a hand speared through the water and grabbed him by the wrist. He screamed as the nails dug into his skin. It tugged him sharply, the entire rowboat tilting until Shelby spun around and slammed the hand with her oar. "HEY! GET OFF!"

The fingers went limp and then slunk away, disappearing underneath the sail.

Fionn curled his hand into his chest. "Thanks," he said to Shelby. He handed the candle back to Sam. "Here. You should hold it again."

Sam took it gingerly. "Oh, yippee."

The memory turned them around and sent them after Hughie Rua. He was advancing without pause, the remaining two ships shouldering themselves to his attack.

He was still laughing.

"He's a *madman*," said Sam.

"I*sn't* he?" said Fionn proudly.

Hughie was back at the bow, with his hands fastened on his hips. He was relishing this. He was *made* for this. And with two pirate ships still bearing down on him, he wasn't one bit afraid.

They followed the path forged by *Saoirse*. The wind was doing most of the work—not that Hughie paid any heed to an empty rowboat swept up in his adventure. There was another ship coming straight for him.

The Mors.

Hughie bared his teeth. "Come on then! Do your worst!"

The Storm Keeper raised his hand and the wind picked up in a sudden, violent gust, nearly lifting Sam clean out of the boat. Fionn tugged him back in by the straps of his life jacket.

Keeping one hand on the mast, Hughie lifted his other to the sky. The clouds sank lower, and with an almighty roar, he threw his head back to the storm and pulled a lightning bolt right out of it.

Fionn, Shelby, and Sam screamed as the bolt leaped from the clouds and skewered *The Mors* right down the middle. It ripped through the sails like a guillotine, setting the entire deck ablaze as it sheared it clean in half. The masts tumbled into the ocean, the ship groaning as it rolled over after them.

Their little rowboat sloshed back and forth, as smoke wafted above the water.

"Did you see that?" gasped Fionn.

"I can't breathe!" yelled Sam.

"I'm in a dream!" said Shelby. "Or maybe a nightmare!"

All of a sudden, the sea fell eerily quiet.

From a bruised cloud, the final ship emerged.

Fionn read the name scrawled on its hull.

The Eversio.

It moved as gracefully as a swan.

Hughie Rua slumped against the mast.

"He's gone really pale," said Shelby.

"He was practically see-through to begin with," said Sam.

"But *look*. He can barely keep his eyes open."

Fionn was still watching the ocean. There was something about that final pirate ship—a strangeness in the way it moved—that was making his skin prickle. It had seen Hughie Rua coming, watching on the sidelines as he drowned its companion vessels with little more than a flick of his magic. And yet it had still chosen to move against the Storm Keeper of Arranmore . . . Just what was so important about this invasion that could send these pirates so readily to their death?

Hughie had grown weak. He managed to make a ball of the wind, pressing it together with his fingers. He slung his hands over his head and fired it toward the last pirate ship. The wind bullet took a bite out of its hull, but *The Eversio* stayed its course, skimming over the waves like a stone on water.

"What's he doing?" muttered Shelby. "Why isn't he using the Tide Summoner?"

All ego and arrogant stupidity, said Tara's voice in Fionn's head.

Glory hog.

Shelby banged the sides of their little boat. "Get up, Hughie!" she screamed. "Use the shell!"

"He can't hear you," said Sam.

Hughie staggered toward the bow. He sent another gust out. Fionn barely felt it on his cheeks as it whizzed past.

The Evorsio dropped anchor, pivoting sharply as the ocean swung it around, a rail of loaded cannons suddenly blinking back at them. Fionn bristled as he caught sight of the captain spinning the ship's wheel. It crossed his vision in a flash—streaks of crimson hair whipping through the air.

He was almost sure he had hallucinated it, until Shelby slammed her hand into his back and rocked him forward.

"Was that . . . *Ivan*?"

The air exploded with cannon fire. The iron balls cut through the water and blew a chunk out of Hughie Rua's sailboat. There was an almighty crack. Several planks of wood fell away, taking the *Saoirse*'s name with it. Hughie was thrown backward, his head slamming into his mast.

"No!" yelled Fionn.

The Evorsio swept closer—close enough that they could all see its captain's face now: dark eyes and narrow shoulders, tattoos crawling like spiders up his bare neck. There could be no confusion now—no room for second thoughts.

"It's really him," gasped Shelby. "And he's *grinning*! *Look*."

Fionn was reeling.

The captain of *The Evorsio* was Ivan.

Ivan had led the invasion of 1728.

The pirates gurgling to their deaths were not humans but a contingency of Soulstalkers, most of them now scattered across the ocean by his ancestor's magic.

"Look! The Tide Summoner!" Sam pointed across the sea, where Hughie Rua had lumbered to his feet. Blood was streaming down his face and pooling in the sides of his mouth. He was trying to remove something from the folds of his shirt.

With an almighty groan, he pulled it free. It was just the size of his huge hand—a spiraling white conch shell, rimmed in glittering gold. Fionn's magic leaped in his chest, flaring white-hot in recognition. In *want*. A small part of him longed to launch himself into the sea and swim toward it.

Hughie braced himself against the mast. "Dagda help me!" he heaved as he lifted the shell to his lips.

The cannons loosed their next assault, the balls whistling past their ears and missing their little boat by less than an arm's length.

Above the thunder clash of an angry sky, the Tide Summoner rang out.

Chapter Twelve

THE TIDE SUMMONER

The song fell upon them like a veil. It was a strange, haunting lament that seemed to stretch time, turning seconds into minutes, minutes to hours, while an invisible finger plucked the strings of their hearts.

Eight waves to call the tide,

On the ninth wave, the merrows ride.

The sea began to swell.

Hughie Rua dropped the shell over the side of the *Saoirse* and slumped against the bow.

"No!" Fionn felt a terrible pull in his chest as the white specter dissolved in the froth, sinking right before his eyes. He leaned over the boat, grasping helplessly at the water.

A sudden surge nearly knocked him into the sea. Shelby grabbed his life jacket and pulled him back. "Let it go, Fionn. We're too far from it!"

"I have to dive for it! It's the reason we're here!"

"Are you crazy?" shouted Sam.

"I can feel it!" Fionn clutched the collar of his life jacket. There was a fire erupting in his chest. "It's here. It's underneath us!"

"You'll lose your link to the memory if you dive in!" Sam tugged on the rope. "If the candle goes out now, we'll all be stranded in the middle of the ocean without a boat!"

"Guys! There's something wrong with Hughie!" yelled Shelby, over another sky-shattering blast. A cannonball tore through the last of the *Saoirse*'s maroon sails.

The waves kept growing, great heaving crests pouring over the horizon and stampeding toward them. A drumbeat pounded in Fionn's ears. It was keeping rhythm with the throbbing sea. Even the ocean knew. Somehow it knew . . .

The merrows were coming.

The Evorsio was knocked off course by a towering surge. Another cannon blast—another chunk torn out of the little sailboat. Hughie had slipped out of view. There was only the tip of his leathered boot now, splayed across the deck. Unmoving.

The sea went still. The ninth wave was sucked down under the water until the surface looked as smooth and shiny as a coin. The sky flashed, the thunder roared, and from the depths of the undersea came the merrows in an explosion of shrieking glory.

A thousand creatures shattered the surface in one endless smear of blue.

They all wore the same yellow eyes and shark teeth, clenched jaws so sharp they could cut glass. Their blade-like cheekbones protruded over hollowed cheeks, but all their tail fins were different—some were coal black and midnight blue, while others glinted tarnished gold and molten amber. Their torsos were honed differently as well, some bare and barely blue, others slashed and spattered by the sea's debris. Some wore their hair like seaweed, long and coarse and matted with shells, but most had none at all, their ears flat and webbed beneath shining heads.

There was one alone that Fionn recognized, and he found her immediately.

Riding at the front of her army, wearing her coral and bone crown, and the most terrifying smile Fionn had ever seen, was Lír, Queen of the merrows. Queen of Terror. She had come to answer Hughie Rua's call, and though Fionn knew now of the Tide Summoner's bond, he couldn't ignore the stab of envy in his gut.

Lír released a savage cry, and Fionn's magic jumped yet again, summoned by a power even greater than the Tide Summoner. Here was the Tide itself—living, breathing warriors, carved from the same ancient force. It felt for an awful second like the magic was trying to leap up his throat and burst from his mouth, to follow her call into war.

Why, he thought angrily, *do you never answer mine?*

The merrows spread themselves in a wide circle, dragging the sea behind them. They surrounded *The Evorsio*, pushing the lone ship back toward the jagged rocks. Away from Fionn. Away from Sam and Shelby. Away from Hughie Rua's unconscious body.

The sky opened in a gash of silver lightning, as the hull of *The Evorsio* splintered against Black Point Rock. Cannons rolled out, denting arms and fins and skulls and faces, as Soulstalkers jumped out after them, taking their chances in the sea. The merrows were on them almost immediately, razing sharp teeth through ancient bone.

"There's Ivan!" shouted Shelby. "He's scrabbling up the mast!"

"He's going to jump onto the rocks!" yelled Sam.

The merrows were dragging their scarred bodies up the sides of the ship, webbed fingers tearing splinters from its hull and snapping wildly at Soulstalkers on their way down. Lír snatched one right out of the sky and broke his neck before he hit the water.

The wind was tugging at the collar of Fionn's life jacket. He looked over his shoulder, to Hughie Rua's sinking boat. "Go and help him," he muttered. "You're supposed to help him."

"Who are you talking to?" said Shelby.

"The island," said Fionn, his eyes on his sinking ancestor. "Why are you taking so long?"

The wind only whistled in his ears, prodding his cheeks with its icy fingers.

"This is ridiculous," said Fionn. "Hughie's going to drown!"

He looked for Lír, but she was lost somewhere in a sea of blood and bone.

"Turn the boat around," he said suddenly. "We have to help him!"

"But we're watching the merrows!" said Sam, brandishing the candle in protest. "*Look!* That one just swallowed a *foot!*"

"It doesn't matter," said Fionn urgently. "We have to save Hughie. It's us. It's supposed to be *us*."

"What are you talking about?" said Sam, bewildered now.

Fionn was already slapping his oar against the waves. "*Quick!* Help me!"

Shelby sprang into action, both of them heaving as they turned the rowboat against the tide. They were impossibly far away—and Hughie was drifting farther from them with every passing second. Panic surged up Fionn's throat until he could barely breathe from it. He dug his oar through the sea, over and over, sweat beading on his brow and magic flaring in his chest, until the waves parted around them. The little boat lunged forward, cutting a course through the froth as the wind flapped at their backs.

"Whoa," said Sam, peering over the side. "How are we moving so fast? Is that you, mate?"

"I don't know," gritted Fionn. "Let's just hurry."

When they reached the sailboat, it was already half sunk in the water. The lip of it drew level with their noses. The bow tipped, and Hughie's lumbering body rolled across the deck.

"What are we going to do?" said Sam. "We can't move him! He's way too big."

Fionn was already on his feet, wobbling. "We're going to have to drag him back to shore with us!"

"But we're all tied together," said Shelby. "It'll be impossible!"

Just as she said it, the sailboat tipped and Hughie Rua rolled out, into the open water. Fionn leaped from the rowboat, and nearly cut himself in half on the rope as it tautened. Shelby and Sam screamed as they slammed against the side of the boat. In the water, Fionn wound his arm around Hughie's broad chest and kicked madly with his legs. The water rose around him, pouring streams into his mouth. "Help," he gurgled. "He's too heavy."

There was a *splat!* from over his shoulder as Shelby jumped out of the boat. Sam followed a half second later, the candle hovering perilously close to the waterline as he landed.

They made a triangle around Hughie, Shelby and Sam taking a leg each, while Fionn kept his arm around Hughie's chest. His ancestor's head flopped back onto his shoulder, his pale skin dotted with an endless constellation of freckles.

"Hurry up!" warned Sam. "The candle's about to go out!"

They pushed and pedaled the water, leaving the merrows shrieking far behind them. When they reached the shore, they rolled Hughie onto the sand and sat back on their haunches, gasping for air. Their lips were blue around the edges, their soaking clothes melded to their skin.

"W-w-well . . . Th-th-that. W-was. Insane," said Fionn through chattering teeth.

Sam held the puddle of wax up just as the flame sputtered out. “I c-c-can’t b-b-b-elieve w-w-we d-d-didn’t d-d-die.”

The wind washed Hughie Rua away. The thunder rumbled after him, taking the flashing sky with it.

“W-w-we s-s-survived,” said Shelby, shaking her head in disbelief. “All of us.”

Chapter Thirteen

THE SOULSTALKER'S RETURN

"Not to sour the mood or anything, but we did fail in our mission. The Tide Summoner is still missing," said Sam, after they had peeled off their sopping life jackets and piled them on the rocks. When they untied themselves from the rope, they were alarmed to find it had frayed to almost nothing in several places. "And I don't think my boots will ever be the same either, if that makes you feel even worse. The suede is ruined."

Fionn was standing at the water's edge. "It's not missing," he said, pointing at the sunken tide. "It's in there."

"By 'there,' do you mean the entire *open ocean*?" said Sam, coming to his side.

Shelby wandered over to them, still clutching the

frayed rope. "It's getting dark. We must have been gone for hours."

"The shell could be in Greenland by now," Sam went on, his eyes narrowing at the waves. "Or Canada. Or Angola. Or Bermuda. Or—"

"Stop naming random places. I already know you're cleverer than me," Fionn interrupted. "It's *our* Tide Summoner. It belongs to the island. Do you know what that means?"

They shook their heads.

"It means it's close by. It *has* to be," said Fionn, with a burst of determination. "And that means we can go back for it."

They stared at the tide. It may have been low, but it was still sprawling.

"The sun is setting . . . ," said Shelby quietly. "And I'm *really* cold."

"I need a hot bath," said Sam. "And a cup of tea."

Fionn wasn't cold or thirsty. He was focused. Somewhere underneath that wide expanse of sea, the Tide Summoner was waiting for them. "We'll come back for it first thing tomorrow then. With more candles this time. A bucketload. Shelby, you and Sam can push the tide out, and I'll search the seabed." He spun around. "This is better anyway. We don't have to steal it from the past. We can lift it right out of the sea. Don't you see? We're so *close*." He gestured vaguely over his shoulder. "It's right *there*, waiting for us."

Fionn could picture Elizabeth Beasley's disappointment so easily now, the disgruntled look on her face the moment she realized he had succeeded without her. Without his own magic, even. He was going to bring glory to his family name. Not shame, or regret. He was going to prove that sour old woman wrong, once and for all.

"I don't know," said Sam uncertainly. "Shelby and I have never used the candles like that."

"It's easy," said Fionn quickly. "Tara says you just have to think about it, and it happens. If the other islanders can do it, then so can you." Fionn was hopping from foot to foot now, imagining the shell wedged and gleaming on the seabed. The same excitement was catching in Sam's eyes—his own chance to use the candle magic, a chance to be a Storm Keeper too.

"I've seen Maggie Patton lift the sea with a flick of her wrist, and a whale along with it," said Fionn. "You have the same blood in your veins—I bet you'd do an excellent job!" He thumped his chest. "I'll be able to feel it once the tide is out. There's a magical pull. It's like something inside me recognizes it."

Sam grinned. "Well, when you put it like—"

"No," Shelby cut in. "We need Tara. *She's* the expert."

"I'm not asking Tara," said Fionn firmly. "She thinks looking for the Tide Summoner is pointless. Besides, she'll hold it over me for the rest of eternity."

"You're being ridiculous!" snapped Shelby suddenly. She blinked, bringing a hand to her throat, as though she had surprised even herself.

Fionn took a step away from her. "No, I'm not," he said in a wounded voice.

"You have to ask your sister, Fionn."

Fionn stared at Shelby, her narrowed eyes and twisting mouth, the sudden shortness of her temper. He hadn't even realized she *had* a temper. "What's got into you?"

"Common *sense*," said Shelby.

"Where was your common sense when we put those ropes around us and threw ourselves into a dangerous pirate invasion?" asked Sam.

Shelby folded her arms. "This is different."

"Don't you want to help us?" asked Fionn.

"No," she said flatly. "Not like this, I don't."

"But—"

"I'm not doing it." She turned around and marched toward the cliffs. "If you're going to mess with the tide, then we need more than just us. Sam and I won't be enough."

Fionn and Sam trailed after her in utter bewilderment.

The way out of the cove was less arduous, now that they had unpinned themselves from each other, but the awkwardness was stifling. Their breathing was too loud in the silence, the three of them huffing and panting as they picked their way up the rocks on their hands and knees. When they reached the top, the sun was already floating on the horizon, and the earth was frozen beneath them.

"Ominous," said Sam, kicking an icy strip of seaweed.

Shelby marched inland, her hair damp and stringy against her back. Fionn jogged after her, signaling for Sam to give them a minute alone. He followed her through a thicket of evergreens and into a deserted field, where he found her sitting on a low wall with her arms pulled around her.

"Shel— Oh," said Fionn, staring at the tears trickling down her cheeks. "What's wrong?"

Shelby kept her eyes on her shoes. "I'm sorry for yelling at you, Fionn. I didn't mean to snap."

"It's fine," said Fionn quickly. "I live with Tara."

Shelby wiped her cheeks with her damp sleeve. "I want to help you tomorrow," she sniffed. "I just . . . *can't*."

Fionn hovered awkwardly. He wasn't sure what to do. When his mother got sad, he would bring her soup or chocolate, sit quietly beside her on the couch—so that she knew he was there—while she watched three consecutive episodes of *Say Yes to the Dress*. When Tara was upset, it was usually due to a boy band breaking up, or the result of something like the last northern white rhino dying, despite her not knowing of its existence until she read an article about its extinction. Usually, he would ignore her for several days. Weeks, if fate allowed it.

This was different. He wanted to make Shelby feel better, but he didn't know what was making her feel bad in the first place.

"Are you scared?" he said quietly. "It's okay if you're scared. I'm scared all the time, actually. But the candle magic is easy, and the tide is so low already, and I know that shell is—"

"I'm not scared," said Shelby, shaking her head.

Fionn waited.

"I just can't use those candles." She wiped a rogue tear away, her voice barely more than a whisper when she said, "I'm not a descendant of Dagda, Fionn."

Fionn blinked at her. "What are you talking about? You're a Beasley."

"Yeah, I am a Beasley, I'm just not one by blood." She waited a beat, watching Fionn's face for dawning understanding.

It didn't come.

"Oh, for heaven's sake, Fionn. I'm adopted! My birth parents weren't from Arranmore."

"Oh." Fionn kept his face very still as he computed this new piece of information.

"Yeah," said Shelby. "That's why I didn't want to light the candle earlier. Probably why the rope nearly split in two when I piggybacked on your adventure."

"Oh," Fionn said again. He could see it now—Shelby didn't look like the other Beasleys. She had a wide mouth that curved at the edges, always smiling even when she didn't mean to. Her nose was small and ski-sloped, not long and thin like Bartley's, and her hair was bright and sandy, as though woven from the shoreline. And—perhaps most importantly—she was inherently kind, not forged from pure, undiluted, ever-sneering evil.

Fionn thought of the summer, the race to the Sea Cave that had nearly seen them all dead. Was that why she never chased the wish? Why she stood back and let Bartley take it, passed it off as a lack of interest in being her grandmother's puppet? Was that why she'd never imagined herself as the Storm Keeper? She was certainly brave enough, *determined* enough. She would have been excellent, in fact. She would have been far better than Fionn . . .

"It doesn't bother me," said Shelby. "Not ever. My parents had Bartley, and then my dad got ill, and he got better again, but the treatment . . . well, it meant they were going to be stuck with just Bartley forever, and they thought it might be better to dilute his personality."

"A great idea," said Fionn.

"So they adopted me. And I enriched their lives beyond belief."

"Obviously," concurred Fionn.

"I know everyone loves me as much as they love Bartley. I think my dad probably loves me *more* than him."

"That does not surprise me."

"It doesn't ever come up." She shrugged. "Except on days like today." She looked down at her Converse, the sparkles now mussed with wet sand. "I want to help you find the shell, but the magic won't work for me, Fionn."

Fionn sat down on the wall beside her. "If it helps, the magic doesn't work for me either. And I'm from *two* bloodlines. At least you're brave. I'm useless *and* a coward."

Shelby smiled weakly. "You're not useless, Fionn."

"Tell that to the islanders."

"They'll see for themselves," said Shelby confidently.

"Dagda was a good sorcerer," said Fionn. "He wouldn't have cared where you were from, only what was in your heart. He would have known how . . . how special you are.

How loyal you are to this place. He would have rewarded you for it."

Shelby's smile faltered. "We don't know that, Fionn. We don't know where he's buried, or what he wanted. We don't know anything about him. Morrigan's awake, and it feels like he's gone for good."

This was not the first time Fionn had thought about this, but it was the first time it had been put to him so plainly. Where *was* Dagda? Why hadn't he woken up too?

"Well, I want you to be a part of this. If you don't help us, we haven't a hope of finding it. We'd probably get distracted or wander off, and Sam would definitely ruin his fancy coat, along with his shoes, and then what would we do?"

Shelby snorted. "He'd never forgive you."

"No," said Fionn solemnly. "If I ask Tara to come and help with the tide, will you help me search for the shell? I don't really want to walk into the sea by myself anyway."

Shelby looked at her hands.

"*Please?*"

"I don't need your pity, you know."

"This isn't pity talking," Fionn assured her. "It's soul-crushing fear and total incompetence."

There was a beat of nothing. Then Shelby smiled. And Fionn smiled too. "Oh, all right then, you don't have to beg. I suppose there is a role for my incredible bravery, after all."

The telltale crunch of footsteps made them snap their heads up. Sam appeared through a break in the trees. "Oh, don't mind me, I'm just wandering around this wintery wilderness, waiting for frostbite to claim me," he announced. "It's not like I *need* my fingers for my future lucrative career in classical music. They can just give me robot hands. By all means, finish your private chitchat."

Shelby leaped to her feet. "Oh, cheer up, cranky-pants, you'll survive," she said, beaming at him.

Sam looked at Shelby. Then at Fionn. "I'm confused."

They made their way back through the evergreens, dodging jagged branches and prickling needles until they reached the path. A lone woman bustled along it, hemmed in by brambles and the spines of headless rosebushes.

They watched her go past. Her back was hunched, her shawl tossed about her head so that her face was hidden. She was quick on her feet, despite the weight that seemed to bend her to the ground.

"Wasn't she . . . ?" Shelby began.

"Is that . . . ?" started Sam.

"That's . . . Rose," said Fionn at the same time.

They were all thinking the same impossible thing—that Rose looked very much like the woman from Hughie Rua's time.

"Go on ahead," said Fionn. "I'll catch up with you."

Sam and Shelby exchanged a glance, then shrugged their way down the path, toward the distant pier.

Fionn trailed after Rose. "Hey," he called. "Can I talk to you for a minute?"

Rose turned around, watching him from the shadows of her shawl. "What is it?"

"I just wanted to thank you," said Fionn, a little awkwardly. "For looking after my grandad, I mean. I see the baskets every week. You did his shopping for him when he stopped being able to leave the house . . . Thank you for taking care of him, even though he's not the Storm Keeper anymore. I—I mean, we—my sister and my mom and I appreciate it."

"You are a Keeper once, you are a Keeper forever." Rose took a step toward him, and he caught the glint of green in her eyes. There was warmth there too. He could feel it spreading inside him, and he felt safer because of it. "All Keepers are special in their own way, but sometimes, Fionn, you can be something else. Something *more*."

Fionn swallowed the sudden dryness in his throat, the jarring feeling that this strange old woman was not looking at him, but *into* him.

"Don't fear what you don't yet know about yourself, Storm Keeper. Your magic will come." She gestured over his shoulder, toward the horizon. "And therein possibility waits side by side with darkness."

She left him staring after her, humming idly to herself while Fionn's mind whirred with more questions than answers.

When he rejoined Sam and Shelby down on the strand, their faces were ashen with fear. Both of them were standing so still, they looked like a couple of damp statues. Wordlessly Sam raised his finger, and Fionn followed it all the way down to the pier, where the evening ferry was pulling in.

Fionn spotted him immediately. One person moving through the droves of passengers, thinking and talking and walking for himself. It was unmistakable—that glimpse of blood-red hair, hovering like a laser-point in the distance.

The horn sounded, and the Soulstalkers parted.

Fionn watched in horror as Ivan stepped off the ferry.

Chapter Fourteen

THE BURNING BOATS

Fionn raced home only to find a holly wreath hanging on the front door. Inside, the cottage looked like Christmas had staggered in and thrown up everywhere. There was tinsel as far as the eye could see, a bowl of striped candy canes in the middle of the kitchen table, and an un-iced fruit cake cooling on the countertop. A giant statue of Santa Claus stood sentry in the hallway, wearing a scarf of blinking fairy lights. There were four stockings hanging above the fireplace, all of them different lengths and colors. On closer inspection, the last one was just an oversized sports sock.

Fionn stalled in the archway to the kitchen.

He had almost forgotten about Christmas.

How could he have forgotten about Christmas?

It was less than a week away. Back in Dublin, it used to be the highlight of his year, the one time when he could ask for a present and not feel bad about it. The one time when Tara made a special effort not to be extremely terrible. She was in the kitchen now, singing to herself as she placed lopsided gingerbread men on a baking tray.

In the sitting room, Fionn's grandfather was jamming an evergreen tree into the corner. Fionn's mother had disappeared somewhere underneath it, her legs poking out as she attempted to screw the bottom of the trunk into a plastic stand.

The tree was swaying back and forth, his grandfather adjusting his stance as his mother's orders climbed up through the branches. "Straighter! No, left! *Left*. Hold! Hold it there, Malachy! Stop swaying! I can feel you swaying!"

Fionn stood and watched his grandfather holding in his laughter as his mother finally emerged from the boughs of the tree with half of its pine needles in her hair. The two of them twirled the tree around to find the fullest angle, arguing over which side was the best one, and whether it should face the window or the sitting room. Fionn's mother laughed as she flicked pine needles at his grandfather, who then pretended to shove them in his mouth and chew them up, *hmm*'ing things like "Surprisingly rustic" and "Could do with a dollop of mustard" while Tara giggled at them from the kitchen.

"Sweetheart." Fionn's mother's face split into a grin. "I didn't hear you come in. How long have you been standing there?"

"Long enough to be shirking off work," said his grandfather, unfolding himself like a greeting card. His eyes were stormless and blue. "Tara says you went off looking for that shell today. We thought we'd prepare Christmas while you were gone. This place was getting awfully grim, and we thought it might cheer you up."

Fionn frowned. "When I failed to find it, you mean?"

"Well, there was no harm in having a look," said his grandfather cheerfully. He lifted a cardboard box from the floor and plunked it on the couch. Dust spiraled from the surface as he raised the lid to reveal a cavalcade of Christmas lights and sparkly baubles, strips of tinsel and little wooden ornaments, thrown haphazardly together. "Come and help me decorate this beast. Your mother has no eye for interiors."

Fionn's mother glared at the back of his head as he rifled through the box. "If you would just let me renovate the place . . ."

"As we have already discussed, Evie, I like my cottage walls drafty and partially exposed," he said, waving his hand behind him dismissively. "It adds a certain authenticity to the whole affair."

In the kitchen, Tara turned her attention on Fionn. "Well? Aren't you going to tell us about your failed adventure?"

"It wasn't a failure," said Fionn, without meeting her eyes.

"Then where's the shell?"

Fionn sighed. He would just have to do it now; he would tell her exactly what happened and then ask for her help. He would endure the horrible smugness of it, and then it would be over, and he could put it behind him.

Their grandfather pulled a wooden figurine out of his box and jabbed it into the air with triumph. "Ta-*da*! Found it!"

"What's that?" asked Fionn, seizing the brief distraction.

I'll do it. I *will,* I *will,* I *will.*

"It's the angel for the top of the tree," said his grandfather.

"Hang on a second." Fionn's mother took the figurine from his grandfather and rotated it in her hand. "Is this . . . *you,* Malachy?"

It was indeed a wooden ornament of Malachy Boyle. The same blue eyes and bald head, the same horn-rimmed glasses sitting on the bridge of his large nose. It was even wearing his favorite blue sweater.

Fionn's grandfather threw his head back and laughed.

"We are not putting *you* on the top of our Christmas tree!" said Fionn's mother. "It's supposed to be an angel, or a star."

"Well, now it's both."

She set the ornament down and tried to chew the smile from the inside of her cheeks. "You are ridiculous."

"Where did that even come from?" said Tara. "It looks like something out of a horror movie. It better not come alive in the night and try to kill us."

"Some of the island kids made it for me in a woodworking class about ten years ago," said Fionn's grandfather, stroking it lovingly. "As a gift for their Storm Keeper. Just *look* at that craftsmanship. I mean, am I looking at a statue, or am I looking in a mirror? I can hardly tell."

Fionn's mother rolled her eyes.

Tara giggled.

"Well," said Fionn, taking it from his grandfather and fixing it in place over the highest branch. "You should put it on top of the tree then."

"All right." Fionn's mother relented. "But we're not having tinsel. It's too garish."

"Booooo," said Malachy. "Who let the Grinch in?"

"And we're not eating the cake until Christmas Day," she added. "I still have to ice it."

"But why?" he said, crestfallen.

"Don't be so heartless, Mom," said Tara. "Surely we can all have a little piece. To taste it."

"Just in case there's arsenic in there," said Fionn's grandfather. "You never know these days."

"Why would I put arsenic in my own Christmas cake, Malachy?"

"Well, I don't know. Why do you drink that God-awful tea?"

"You have *got* to stop nagging me about that," she muttered.

"I can't and I won't. It's far from fancy tea you were raised on, Evelyn McCauley, and I won't let you forget it."

Fionn stood back from the tree and watched the little statue of his grandfather twirl round and round, tugged by an invisible breeze.

His mother came to his side. "Don't be too disappointed about this shell business, love. It was such a long shot to begin with."

Tara prodded him in the arm. "You hardly thought you'd *actually* track it down, did you?"

"I *did* track it down," said Fionn. "In fact, I know exactly where it is."

Fionn's mother blinked in surprise.

"*Really*?" said Tara skeptically.

"Yes, really," said Fionn seriously.

Fionn's grandfather looked up from his decorating. "You mean you've seen it?"

Fionn nodded. "Sam, Shelby, and I burned the *Saoirse* candle today. We went back to the pirate invasion and followed Hughie Rua out of the cove. We saw him use the Tide Summoner. We *heard* it. And then we saw him drop it into the sea afterward too."

"You did *what*?" said Tara, aghast.

Fionn's mother pressed a hand to her collarbone. "Fionn, you could have *died*."

Fionn's grandfather laid down the bauble he was holding. "Goodness."

Fionn turned to his sister and before he could lose his nerve, he forced the words out. "I know *where* the Tide Summoner is. More or less. I just . . . I need your help to get it."

THUMP, THUMP, THUMP!

Fionn jumped. "Don't answer it," he said, shooing them away from the door. "I think it's Ivan."

"*Ivan?*" said his grandfather with alarm.

"Why would it be Ivan?" said Fionn's mother. "He's not back on Arranmore. Is *he?*"

Tara jabbed him in the ribs. "Fionn?" she hissed. "What's going on?"

THUMP, THUMP, THUMP!

This time, they all jumped.

"I know you're in there! I can hear the chatter!" came a familiar voice through the door. "It's Donal! Can you open the door?"

Fionn's mother swung the door open and Donal bustled into the cottage, his skin paler than his hair. "Come quickly," he said, grabbing Fionn by the shoulders. "There's no more time to waste." He pulled him toward the open door. "They're gathering down on the beach. Everything was quiet and then all of a sudden that last ferry arrived and they crawled out of the ground like insects!" He caught a panicked breath and swallowed it down with a gulp. "They've ransacked the shop and upended the pub. Now they're burning all the fishing boats."

Fionn was already re-buttoning his damp coat. "Let's go!"

Fionn's mother was at the coatrack in a flash, wrapping herself up. "Will you be okay here by yourself, Malachy?"

"I'll use the candles if anything crawls up this way," said Fionn's grandfather. "Though let me tell you, it'll be the last thing they do."

Tara was already stuffing her coat with candles. Their grandfather was helping her, shoving them in three at a time. "Don't reveal the magic unless you're in direct danger," he warned her. "Stick together. Buy more time. See what they want. If Fionn really has found the shell, then every hour from now counts. Be *smart*."

They bustled out onto the headland, following Donal into an unforgiving winter. Crystals hung from the trees, swaying precariously in the wind. The flowers were coated in frost, their colored heads lost to the plummeting temperature.

Fionn smelled the smoke before he saw the flames. The fishing boats were burning, all of them lined up along the dwindling tide, spitting dark fumes into the sky. The islanders were huddled on the roadway, their backs to Donal's looted shop, to the post office and the ransacked pub with all its lights still on. On the bridge, Sam and his family were watching the commotion too.

Niall and Alva spotted Fionn immediately, weaving through the panicked crowds until they reached him.

"There's no plan for this," said Niall, glancing over his shoulder. "Our final meeting isn't until tomorrow. We're not prepared."

"We need more time," said Alva, her breath stuttering. "We still have children here. And elderly."

"It's all right, Alva," said Fionn's mother, taking her by the arm and squeezing tight so her own hands wouldn't shake. "Let's just figure out what's going on first."

Niall set his mouth in a hard line. "It seems clear to me, Evie. They have their commander here now. They're following orders."

Fionn scanned the length of the strand, picking out Ivan just as he stepped away from his army and raised his hand in the air.

The Soulstalkers fell deathly quiet.

Up on the roadway, the islanders did too.

"Dwellers of Arranmore, Descendants of *Dagda*," said Ivan in a loud, gleeful voice. "Your fate lies now in my hands. Your Storm Keeper has failed to protect you. Your island is no longer your own. The old world has returned to Arranmore, and it answers only to me."

Fionn ducked away from the others and pushed through a sea of shoulders until he stood at the very forefront of the islanders.

Ivan took a step toward him. "Your island has buckled under the failure of your leader, and now he must pay the price."

Another step.

"The winter solstice falls tomorrow night. At sunset, I will return to this beach. If you give me the Storm Keeper, I will spare you your lives—and those of your animals. That is my first and final offer. Refuse, and you will see those you love perish before your eyes. Choose to protect the person who has failed to protect you, and you will spend the rest of your days drowning in the blood of those you hold dearest."

There was an awful stretch of silence. Nobody moved. Nobody breathed. Not even Fionn.

"Sundown tomorrow," Ivan repeated. "Your fate is one. The island will live or die together."

He raised his hands and clicked his fingers. Over his shoulder an almighty explosion ripped a hole in the sky. All the stars went out, the clouds turned to plumes of black and gray as both ferry boats went up in a torrent of flames. The sea bled red and orange as metal rained down on the strand.

The islanders scattered, screaming as they covered their heads.

The Soulstalkers roared with laughter. One unending robotic laugh that rattled all the way through Fionn's bones.

Tara tore through the chaos with a candle raised to the sky. "I'll drown him!" she screamed. "Let me try! Just let me try!"

Fionn lunged for Tara. "No!" he hissed, pulling her back. "It won't be enough! Don't show him our magic. We have to save it. We have to *plan*!"

Tara was panting so hard, she could barely speak. "*What* plan? We don't have one, Fionn!"

"We do!" he said, dragging her back, with the help of his mother. "If all goes well, we'll have the shell by sundown tomorrow. We can blow it when all of his creepy minions are standing on that beach, and use the candles to keep them there—right where we want them. The merrows will chew them up before they can even open their mouths to scream. It's perfect, really."

"Listen to your brother," said Fionn's mother urgently. "There's a smarter way than this."

"Take my message and carry it throughout the island," Ivan called after them, the flames still rising at his back. "Spread word to those too afraid to leave their homes tonight, to the people who believe that looking away from the fire will stop it from burning. Find the measure of your courage—what are you willing to do to save yourself? Will you sacrifice the boy who has been sacrificing you? Perhaps you won't have to think too hard, after all. Tick-tock, Arranmore."

Tick-tock, Storm Keeper.

Tick-tock, here's *the Reaper.*

Back at *Tír na nÓg*, Fionn's grandfather listened to their account with uncharacteristic gravitas. "It's clever, isn't it?" he muttered, pacing the length of the room. "He's only just arrived and he's sowing dissension in our ranks. Cutting off our options. *Burning* them.

Blaming Fionn. He's isolating the lad so he'll be easier to pick off."

"I'll wring his scrawny neck," fumed Tara.

Fionn blinked at her.

"What?" she said, folding her arms. "Only I'*m* allowed to be mean to you."

Fionn's mother had taken to her phone, her fingers flying across the screen so fast they turned blurry. "I've been talking to Alva and Phil and the others," she said without looking up. "We're meeting tomorrow in the school hall to arrange our plan of attack."

"Good," said Fionn's grandfather. "That's the island way."

"Yeah," echoed Tara, a tremor in her voice. "Good."

"They'll want to hear from Fionn," said Fionn's mother, her eyes still on her phone. "He's our leader, after all."

Fionn ignored the hollowness in that word—*leader.* He was just as afraid as the rest of them, but he was determined not to show it. "Tara and I can get up at sunrise and go back to Hughie Rua's Cove," he said, pacing the room too. "The shell is on the seabed, somewhere between the beach and Black Point Rock. I have a pretty good idea of where it went down. When we push the tide out, I should be able to find it. Then we can bring it to the island meeting and show everyone."

"Stage a false handover with Ivan on the beach at

sundown," said his grandfather, picking up the thread of his plan.

"Then blow the shell and drown the Soulstalkers," said Fionn.

"And use the candles to stop the ones that try to get away!" said Tara excitedly.

"Excellent plan," said their grandfather approvingly. "You'd make a fantastic bank robber, Fionn."

"And if we *don't* find the shell?" said Fionn's mother, looking up from her phone. "Just in case something goes wrong, what then?"

Fionn stared at the candles in their midst, reams of unused wax simmering with secret magic. He thought of all the islanders who would have to risk their lives against Ivan's promised barbarity and felt a sharp pain in his gut. "We'll cross that bridge if we come to it."

They fell into silence, lost to their own thoughts—visions of what might unfold in the morning light, of the future fragile as an eggshell in their hands. When night fell in earnest, and the smoky sky crept up over the headland and down the chimney at *Tír na nÓg*, Fionn's mother suggested that they all set up camp in the living room. It would be a way to keep watch over each other, and Fionn most especially, until dawn broke. Until the lingering scent of the ferry-boat explosion finally passed over them.

She laid out three sleeping bags on the sitting-room floor, piling them with enough pillows and blankets to reach halfway to the ceiling. Tara arranged a bunch of candles and lighters around them, just in case Ivan or his cronies decided to pay them a visit in the night.

Fionn surrendered the couch to his mother, his grandfather insisting on sleeping on the floor, "like the good old days at American summer camps I never went to." He made his bed beside the fire grate, the glowing embers casting a soft glow about his face. Fionn slept head to toe with Tara, her feet twitching perilously close to his nose, until he had scooted so far across the room his head ended up under the Christmas tree.

Tara was the first to fall asleep, her nose-whistle breath whinnying in the silence. His mother dropped off soon after, flinging her arm down the side of the couch. Her breathing deepened, until she sounded like an elephant giving birth. Fionn lay in the dark and stared very hard at the ceiling.

"Fionn?" whispered his grandfather after a while.

"Yeah?" Fionn whispered back.

"If I sterilize a kitchen knife, will you please cut my ears off?"

Fionn smiled. "Only if you promise to cut mine off afterward."

His grandfather chuckled.

A few minutes later, he spoke again. "Are you afraid, lad?"

"I'm always afraid," said Fionn. "Aren't you?"

"Not a bit. Let the Soulstalkers come. They'll only live to regret it." His grandfather *hmm*'d under his breath. "Actually, they won't be able to regret it because they will be dead."

"Right," said Fionn.

"Dead because I will have killed them," he clarified.

"Yeah, I got that."

"And it will be a gruesome, gruesome end."

Fionn's smile dissolved in the silence. "How come you're so brave all the time?"

"Because I love you more than I fear them, Fionn."

Fionn blew out a breath. He could feel his heartbeat fluttering beneath his collarbone, like a trapped bird. "You're very wise, Grandad."

"And?"

Fionn rolled his eyes in the darkness. "And handsome."

A few minutes later, his grandfather's snores joined the chorus around him, a deep baritone in an orchestra of nightmares.

Chapter Fifteen

THE MAKESHIFT PRISON

Fionn lay awake for another hour, until inky fingers smudged the moon from the sky and scattered clouds across the stars.

When he finally slipped into unconsciousness, Morrigan was there, waiting for him.

I *have a place for you in the darkness, Storm Keeper.*

I *have a place for you beside me.*

Then came the laughter, rocking him by the shoulders, pulling him by the hair, stuffing fists down his throat and stealing the air from his lungs.

Tick-tock, tick-tock, tick-tock, tick-tock, tick—

"FIONN!"

Fionn sat bolt upright and smashed his head against

a Christmas bauble. There were pine needles in his hair, pine needles on his cheeks, a pine needle in his mouth. He spat it out, blinking through a mass of green and red and gold as he unearthed himself from the tree.

Tara was standing in front of him. "You sleep like the dead."

I *sleep* with *the dead*, thought Fionn.

"Shelby and Sam are here."

She stood back, and Fionn noticed his friends hovering directly behind her. "What time is it?"

"7:47 a.m.," said Sam. "And *freezing*."

Fionn grabbed his blanket and pulled it over his shoulders. He was suddenly conscious of his spaceship pajama bottoms, the Avengers T-shirt that was two sizes too small for him now. "I must have slept through my alarm," he croaked. "Sorry."

"Probably the fumes," said Shelby, gesturing at the chimney. "Our house smelled like smoke all night, thanks to Ivan's explosion."

"You should hurry up and get dressed," said Sam nervously. "We have a little problem."

"I'd say medium-size," called Fionn's grandfather from inside the kitchen. He was still in his pajamas, staring out the window with a cup of tea in one hand. Fionn's mother hovered beside him, glaring at something in the garden. "Nothing a bit of ingenuity won't fix, I'm sure."

Fionn rubbed the sleep from his eyes as he crossed the room. "What are you talking about?"

He paused at the sound of a toilet flushing. "What was that?" he said, spinning around. "Who else is here?"

The bathroom door shut and two seconds later, Bartley Beasley came striding into the sitting room. A navy sweater peeked over the edge of a gray tailored coat and, as always, he was wearing deck shoes, despite the noted absence of a summer yacht in the French Riviera. He looked less like a teenager and more like a middle-aged banker from Dublin City; the hair on his head swirled like a ninety-nine-cent ice-cream cone. "Nice T-shirt, Boyle."

Fionn stiffened. "This is *way* bigger than a medium-size problem."

Tara rolled her eyes. "Bartley's not the problem, Fionn."

"What's he doing here?" said Fionn, ignoring her.

"Mom and Dad wouldn't let me come here on my own," said Shelby apologetically.

"I snuck out," said Sam proudly.

"And we *need* Bartley," Tara added. "You hardly thought I could drag the sea all by myself?"

Sam pointed at himself. "A*hem* . . ."

"And you're always going on about how good you are with the candles," said Fionn.

"I *am* good." Tara folded her arms. "But I'm not Dagda, for goodness sake! It'll take three of us at least, and we can't leave Grandad here all by himself. Mom has to stay with him."

Fionn's mother was still pressed up against the window, murmuring something to his grandfather.

Bartley leered at Fionn. "You heard her, Boyle. You *need* me to save the island. I mean, I can't say I'm not surprised, but I didn't think you'd leave it so last-minute."

"I was waiting to see if you'd come back to welcome Ivan home first," said Fionn. "Maybe bake him an apple pie."

"Fionn!" said Tara and Shelby at the same time.

Fionn stalked past Bartley, joining his mother and his grandfather in the kitchen. "What are you two staring at?"

Fionn's grandfather shuffled to the side. "See for yourself."

Fionn pressed his nose against the glass. Outside, the sky was white as snow, the ground coated in a glistening layer of ice. The grass was sharp with frost, and covered in sunken footprints.

Fionn stiffened.

The footsteps belonged to Soulstalkers. The cottage was surrounded. He could see ten waiting at the front of the house alone, but there were probably double that many out on the headland, and countless more around the back too.

"They let us in fine," said Shelby from over Fionn's shoulder. "Barely even glanced our way, actually."

"They're not interested in our movements," said Fionn's grandfather gravely. "They're only here for Fionn."

Fionn narrowed his eyes at the blank-faced Soulstalkers. They had been stationed like soldiers, not, it seemed, to keep people out. But to keep people in.

To keep *him* in.

"Oh." The word fogged against the glass.

When he pulled back, his grandfather was at the sink, his cup drained of tea. "Don't worry," he said, his eyes alight with a familiar spark of mischief. "I have a plan."

Chapter Sixteen

ESCAPE BY CANDLELIGHT

Fionn hovered in the middle of the sitting room, with his coat zipped up to his chin and his hat pulled low over his ears, while his grandfather handed out candles. The first, *Snowy Christmas 2002*, went to Shelby and Bartley. It was short and squat and milk-bottle white.

"Keep this in your pocket until you're out of sight of the Soulstalkers," he told them. "Then light it and hold on tight to each other. It will be snowing heavily in this layer, so make sure you keep your bearings. Turn around and track north, past the cottage and along the coast, until you get to Hughie Rua's Cove. Shelby knows where to go. Once you find it, blow out your candle, and wait for the others."

Shelby and Bartley looked at each other and nodded.

"Right," said Shelby to Fionn and Sam. "See you soon then."

"Be safe," said Fionn.

"Be smart," said Tara to Bartley. "We'll be right behind you."

They swung the door open and shuffled outside in their winter coats, the candle hidden in Bartley's back pocket. Fionn watched through the sitting-room window until they had disappeared through the front gates and out onto the headland.

The Soulstalkers barely glanced at them as they went. Fionn highly doubted they would have bothered following Bartley and Shelby to the cove in the first place, but it was better to be sneaky than sorry. Secrecy was everything now.

When Fionn turned around, his grandfather was brandishing another candle. *Foggy Easter* was the exact size and shape of an Easter egg, its golden outer coat glossy in the half-light.

"Same story, love," his grandfather told Tara. "Take the candle with you until you're clear of the Soulstalkers. Light it up when you're alone. Then turn around and head north in your new layer." He looked at Sam. "Try not to let the wind turn you around too much. You remember where the cove is, don't you, lad? It'll be awfully foggy, so don't wander too close to the cliffs."

Sam smiled sheepishly. "I'll do my best."

Fionn's grandfather laid a steadying hand on his shoulder. "Do better than that, or Morrigan's shadow will return and devour us all whole, screaming and bleeding from our ears." He patted him on the side of the head, smiling broadly. "All right then. Off you go. Have fun!"

Fionn handed Tara the backpack full of candles. She hitched it onto her back and tightened the straps. "I'll get these there in one piece." She jerked her chin at Sam. "Him too."

"Cheers," said Sam, with none of his usual bravado.

"Get each other there," said Fionn's mother, guiding them toward the front door. "Just keep your heads down, and don't look at the Soulstalkers. If they give you any trouble, I'll go out there and smash a kitchen chair over their heads."

"*Evie*." Fionn's grandfather whistled under his breath. "*That's* the spirit!"

And then Tara and Sam were out of the door, chattering too loudly as they made their way down the garden path, trying not to return the attention of the Soulstalkers who watched them go by. Fionn held his breath until his sister and his friend had disappeared from view, only exhaling when the Soulstalkers returned their attention to the front door.

“Okay, lad. You’re the tricky one.”

Fionn spun around. “They definitely won’t let me leave like that.”

His grandfather nodded. “You’ll have to light your candle inside the cottage.”

“He can be seen in all layers,” Fionn’s mother reminded him. “We have to make sure the cottage is empty in the one he travels to. Otherwise, you might die of a heart attack, Malachy, twenty years before now.”

“Now wouldn’t that be a *scandal*?” said Fionn’s grandfather, wandering from the room. “I’ll be back in a second.”

“Or Cormac will get the fright of his life if you pop up in front of him.” Fionn’s mother smiled sadly. “All of these possibilities at our fingertips, and who knows how many different ways we could hurt ourselves using them.”

“I’ll be careful,” Fionn reassured her.

There was a knock at the windowpane. They jumped as a Soulstalker pressed his face up against the glass. He tapped again, his nose stubbed so they could see his gaping nostrils, his dirty fingernails rolling back and forth.

Fionn’s mother thumped her fist against the glass.

"GET OUT OF HERE, YOU DISGUSTING SOULLESS CRETIN, OR I'LL COME OUT THERE AND BREAK YOUR SPINE!"

The Soulstalker looked past her, to where Fionn was standing by the couch. Then he wandered away from the window and back to his post in the garden.

"They're just trying to scare us," said Fionn's mother, glaring after him.

"Making sure I'm still here, I bet," said Fionn, backing away from the window. "Ivan won't leave anything to chance."

"Well, they've seen you now. Come on." Fionn's mother led Fionn into the hallway, shutting the door behind them. They stood in the dark and waited for his grandfather to come out of his room.

He returned presently, with a candle Fionn had seen many times before. *Record High Tide 1982*—small, simple, and ocean blue. Fionn took it from him and rolled it between his fingers. "Why this one?"

"Because I remember it," said his grandfather simply. "Over time, most of the candle details have slipped away from me. I don't know where I was or what I was doing on any given day. Not this one, though. The tide was so high, it flooded the pier. I was down on the lifeboats, helping passengers off the ferry. Your father was with me. He was around your age then. He couldn't get enough of the boats, rain, hail, or shine. He loved the adventure of it, even if it soaked him to the bone." He smiled to himself, the memory playing behind his eyes. "We were gone for the whole day."

"What about Winnie?" asked Fionn's mother.

"In bed with the flu," he said, chuckling to himself. "She was so delirious, I managed to convince her I was Elton John when I came home singing 'Rocket Man.' I've never seen her so in love."

Fionn pulled a lighter from his pocket. "I'll keep it burning until I'm safely away from the cottage. And then I'll keep my head down and move quickly, so no one notices me."

"Save the end of the candle so you can get back inside later," said his grandfather.

"I will."

"Good lad," said his grandfather, ushering them both inside the little spare room, where Tara and his mother usually slept. It was like stepping into a furniture catalog. The beds sat side by side beneath floral duvets, each one neatly made, with pillows plumped to perfection. Every article of clothing had been folded carefully away in a wooden chest of drawers, crowned by a basket of dried flowers that filled the room with the smell of lavender. Even their shoes were lined up neatly by the window sill.

Fionn's mother closed the curtains. "I really don't like that he's going by himself, Malachy. What if the island kicks him out of the memory? What if the Soulstalkers catch him while the layers are changing? What if—"

"It's all right, Mom," said Fionn, trying not to think about all the ways it could go wrong. "I'll make sure the island has changed before I go outside. It isn't the first time I've been in a memory alone." He was reminded, with sudden sharpness, of his mother standing in the sea with her hands around her belly, screaming for his father. Screaming at the island. "You just stay here, and stay safe. Make the house look lived-in, remember? Otherwise the Soulstalkers will come looking for me and that will ruin everything."

There was a strained silence.

"Evie," said Fionn's grandfather gently. "This is the Storm Keeper's job. It's up to Fionn now."

Fionn's mother's eyes darkened with thoughts he couldn't guess at. She pinched the bridge of her nose. "Well, I still don't have to like it. I don't have to *smile* about it. This cruel, *cruel* place."

"Evie . . ."

She shook her head. "I know, Malachy, I know. You don't have to say it."

Fionn raised the flame to the candlewick. "It's now

or never," he said, his fingers trembling, just a little. "Wish me luck."

The candle lit up, and the wind whipped around Fionn, erasing his family from where they stood, until there was nothing left but the echo of their goodbye.

Fionn stood alone in a bedroom that was rapidly changing underneath his feet. The wind tornadoed around him, but he gritted his teeth and held on to the narrow doorframe.

The walls changed first—winking from white to mint green, the plaster peeling beneath posters of musicians Fionn didn't recognize—crazy hair and leather pants, mouths open mid-song—as their corners fluttered in the wind. His sister's bed disappeared, until there was only one sitting in the middle of the room. Crookedly. The sheets were crumpled, the duvet trailing onto the floor by a dog-eared comic book. *X-Men*—Fionn had to stop himself from reaching for it. The socks came last, springing up one by one by one, until they littered the floor like bombs.

The island exhaled, and Fionn released the doorframe finger by finger and stepped cautiously into the room. His father's room. His father who had been a boy once, like him.

Musical. Nerdy. *Messy.*

Fionn smiled.

The wind grasped at his wrists, but he shook it off and took another step. He traced the pile of comic books on the nightstand, smiled at the empty candy wrappers. There was a cloudy vase sitting on the windowsill. A host of purple forget-me-nots turned to peer at him. The door behind him swung on its hinges, as if to usher him out. For some reason, the island didn't want him in here.

Outside, it was lashing rain, the whole sky pouring itself over the cottage, like a waterfall. Fionn could hear the island's warning in every determined *plink!*

Get out, get out, get out.

But Fionn was standing in a treasure chest of memories—and he would never be here again, not for as long as he lived.

Just one more minute.

There was a blue sweater slung over the radiator. It flapped in the wind, the windows shaking in their frames as Fionn stared at the smudge of chocolate around its collar, the ink stain blooming on the sleeve.

The candle wax began to melt along his fingers.

Reluctantly Fionn turned from the window. "All right," he muttered. "I'm leaving."

The floorboards creaked, and from the dusky hallway came a woman's voice. "Cormac, love? Is that you?"

Fionn froze with his back to the bedroom door. *Oh no.*

He clutched the candle tight against his chest and held his breath, as his grandmother wandered down the little hallway. "Cormac?"

Fionn cursed himself. The island had warned him, but he hadn't listened.

A drop of wax passed over his fingers and landed on the floorboards. A tiny *splat!*

He felt her move into the doorway behind him, sensed her gaze on the back of his head. "What are you still doing here, love? I thought you were going down to the boats to help Dad."

Fionn's heartbeat was so loud, it drowned out the rain. That voice. *Her* voice. So warm and soft and near. It *ached*, the nearness of her. He cleared his throat. "I . . ."

His grandmother laughed—it was a deep, rasping sound that seemed to leap out of her. A *pirate's laugh*, his mother used to say, and as Fionn stood there, frozen in the dazzling sunlight of his grandmother's amusement, he felt it fold itself around his heart. "Oh, I don't blame you, love," she said, chuckling. "I wouldn't be out in this awful rain either. Even if I wasn't half killed with this flu."

She melted back into the hallway, wheezing as she went. "Will you pop down for a while at least? I know he'd love your company. Take the good umbrella." Her bedroom door closed, her voice muffled on the other side of it. "My treat."

Fionn glanced over his shoulder, to the empty doorframe, and felt himself deflate with relief. He hurried into the kitchen, the candle warm in his fist, and slipped out of the front door into an onslaught of rain. There were no Soulstalkers in this layer—no islanders at all, in fact—just the comforting howl of the wind as it came after him, the tide so high he could see it over the cliffs. He jogged out onto the headland and turned north, tracking along the coast, until he was far from the little cottage on the headland and the goons Ivan had dispatched to keep him there.

When he reached the edge of Hughie Rua's Cove, Fionn blew his candle out and stuck the last of it in his pocket. The rain sputtered to a stop, the clouds blown over the horizon in a single gust. The tide crawled back out to sea until the strand emerged in a brassy crescent.

There, just below him, his four fellow adventurers stood side by side.

"Fionn!" Shelby waved her arms back and forth. "You made it!"

"You took *ages*," yelled Tara. "Hurry up!"

Fionn's head was still full of his grandmother's laugh, his heart still full of missing her. Of never truly knowing her. But there was a task at hand, and they were late already. He waved back at his friends, before slipping down the rocks on his hands and knees.

When he reached the bottom of the cove, they faced the tide together. Shelby drew an imaginary line from the sand to the three black rocks, tracing the search area with her finger, while Tara hovered beside her, flicking her bottom lip. "With the tide this low, we should be able to push it all the way back to Black Point Rock. You'll have to be quick though." She glanced at Fionn. "Do you think you'll feel it when you're near?"

"I hope so," said Fionn uneasily. "Seeing as the entire plan hinges on it."

"We'll find it," said Shelby, smiling confidently. "Just make sure we don't drown out there."

"Don't worry," said Sam, flexing his fingers. "I always excel at things on the first try."

"Really?" said Shelby.

Sam nodded. "I was the youngest-ever member of the London Symphony Orchestra."

Bartley turned on him. "What age were you?" he asked accusingly.

"Minus three months," said Sam proudly. "My mom was pregnant with me at the time."

Bartley rolled his eyes. "That obviously doesn't count."

"Jealous," muttered Sam.

"A little focus, please." Tara flung the schoolbag from her back and dumped the candles out onto the beach. They got onto their knees and pulled the anchors out, ripping the silver discs from the bottom of the candles so that the wicks unfurled from the opposite end.

Shelby grabbed the life jackets from where they had left them on the rocks yesterday and handed one to Fionn. "Probably a good idea," she said, slipping it over her head. "Not that I don't trust our siblings."

After a brief tutorial, where Sam did, in fact, excel with the Storm Keeper's magic, Tara positioned the three of them at the edge of the ocean, where they each lit their candles at the same time. Sam laughed giddily as the magic slammed into him, Tara lifted her chin to the sky, and Bartley went rigid as a rod.

They held their arms out, palms up, like the first step in a choreographed dance. There was no sign of outward effort, save for the vein pulsing on Bartley's forehead and the muscle straining in Sam's jaw. The shoreline rolled backward. It looked just as if the tide was going out, the waves receding inch by inch, then foot by foot.

"*Cool*," whispered Shelby.

Fionn tried to ignore the familiar prickles of jealousy. Shelby was right; it *was* cool, even if he wasn't the one doing it. Even if he *should* be the one doing it. Hughie Rua would have ripped the sea up like a carpet, without breaking a sweat. Maggie Patton would have rolled it back on itself like a Fruit Winder. Dagda would have split the entire ocean in two.

Shelby took him by the arm. "Ready?"

The ocean floor appeared before them—cockleshells and clumps of seaweed, scuttling crabs and fish flapping helplessly along the strand. Fionn picked one up by its tail and flung it into the sea. "Ready," he said.

Chapter Seventeen

THE EMPTY TOMB

Fionn and Shelby stepped over the old waterline, and the smell slammed into them. It was like opening an old can of tuna and drowning in that first pungent whiff. Slowly, cautiously, they dropped their hands from their noses and wiped the tears from their eyes. The sea rolled backward and they walked on, emboldened.

The wind deserted them, but there was a stubborn chill in the air. It was even colder in the gullet of the ocean, without the water to blanket it. Shelby bent down to unearth an oyster from the seabed. She brushed her thumb against its ridges, before laying it back down, lovingly. On either side of the cove, frothy waves peered over as though looking to see what they were doing. "Feel anything yet?" she asked him.

Fionn closed his eyes and rubbed circles over his chest. There was a kernel glowing there, an invisible thread tugging him farther into the ocean. "Yeah," he said, pointing toward the sea stacks. "I think it's over there somewhere."

Black Point Rock was still a distance away, but an old shipwreck was emerging just up ahead. The tide retreated, revealing the skeleton of a rotting hull.

"That's not one of Ivan's, is it?" asked Fionn, slowing to examine it.

Shelby shook her head. "It's way too close to the strand. I bet it's one of the Spanish Armada."

They circled the wreck. Shards stuck out of the sand like signposts, the wood soft and chewy where the ocean had been licking at it. "What were the Spanish doing here?" asked Fionn.

"They were sailing to England to overthrow the Queen back in, like, the sixteenth century. But it didn't go well, so they came around the top of Ireland and ran aground on the rocks." Shelby chewed on her bottom lip. "Bad weather. A storm, I think."

It was always a storm.

"It might be *La Juliana*," said Shelby. "Admiral Fernando Aguero jumped right off his sinking ship and swam to shore, and all the local girls here threw themselves at his feet because he was so handsome. He didn't speak a lick of English and none of them spoke Spanish, but he fell in love with an islander and stayed anyway. That's what Mia Aguero told me. Her sister was named after his ship."

"Oh, to be named after a sunken ship," said Fionn wistfully.

Shelby smiled. "Cool origin."

"Almost as cool as ours," said Fionn.

"Yours, you mean," said Shelby, wandering away from the wreck. "We should keep moving."

The seabed dipped, leading them down a slope pocked with rusty cannonballs. Fionn glanced over his shoulder every so often, watching for the others on the shoreline. They were still standing with their palms outstretched. Still within shouting distance. The kernel in his chest was getting warmer, the unseen thread growing taut. "I think we're getting close."

The ocean crept back, back, back, until it loosened the three black rocks from its watery grip. They loomed over them like skyscrapers. A strange sense of unease came upon Fionn as they drifted closer. The heat inside him dimmed and, in its place, nausea bloomed. "Ugh," he said, clutching his stomach.

Beside him, Shelby was doing the same. "I feel a little bit sick."

"We've used nearly half the candles!" came Tara's voice from far away. "Hurry up! Sam's starting to flag!"

Neither Fionn nor Shelby turned around. The sand was vibrating underneath them as though, deep underground, an earthquake was beginning. They stepped over the ripples and stopped at the first rock. Without meaning to, Fionn placed his palm against it. Pain exploded in his head, as sharp and sudden as a thunderbolt. It shot down his arms and spasmed in his chest, until it felt like he was being split in half.

There was a terrible, earth-shattering scream. It took Fionn a moment to realize it was his own. Another moment to realize he was on his knees.

"Fionn!" Shelby hoisted him up by his elbow. "Get away from it!"

Fionn staggered backward, blinking at the rock. There was a shadow moving inside it, like an eel underwater. "Do you see that?"

"I see it," said Shelby, her fingers tightening around his arm.

The shadow leaped toward them, pressing its face against the inside of the rock. Shelby screamed. Fionn stumbled away from it, pulling her with him. "D-d-don't look."

"What *is* that?" said Shelby breathlessly.

They could still see the wide, hulking figure beating

its fists against the rock. Fionn could taste dark magic in the air. He had felt it once before—deep in the belly of the ancient Sea Cave.

"I think it's some kind of tomb," whispered Fionn.

They crept toward the second shard, close enough to see another figure moving in the rock. This one was smaller and narrower than the first. It kept its fists to itself too—silent as a ghost, but quick as an adder as it flitted in and out of the shadows.

Shelby groaned. "They're making me dizzy."

They edged toward the last shard. The strange darkness filtered away, the air clearing until they could breathe properly again. They released their stomachs and filled their lungs. Fionn could feel the kernel glowing in his chest again, sensed the pull of the Tide Summoner somewhere close by.

"This one isn't so bad," said Shelby, creeping closer.

Fionn pointed at the far side of the rock, where a gaping hole traced the length of the shard. "That's because it's empty."

He drifted toward the entrance.

"Fionn! Get back!"

"I want to look inside."

"We're supposed to be looking for the shell!" said Shelby, marching after him.

"It might be in here," he lied. The heat inside him dimmed as he moved away from the Tide Summoner, toward the lingering darkness. With his feet planted firmly on the seabed and his hands on either side of the onyx rock, Fionn stuck his head inside the hole. It was deadly silent and almost black, save for the hundreds of amber gemstones set into the rock. They cast an eerie luminescence about the tomb. "Hello?" he called into the emptiness.

Hello-hello-hello, the emptiness called back.

There was a lone *kra-aaa* from somewhere in the darkness.

The walls blinked.

Amber to black, and then back to amber.

Fionn heard the sudden thwack of wings and stumbled backward, falling over Shelby in his haste to escape. The rock shuddered as it spat out its ravens. They poured over Fionn in an onslaught of shrieking feathers, pecking and *kraaa*-ing as they deserted their tomb and launched themselves across the exposed seabed. Shelby covered her head and screamed, the sound dying in her throat only when the final raven had soared over them.

They scrabbled to their feet, Fionn saying "Sorry, sorry, sorry" as they retreated from the rock. Shelby gathered herself up and wiped the tears from her eyes.

With her bottom lip still trembling, she pointed ahead of them, to where the ocean had been tugged away. "Fionn. *Look!*"

Fionn turned to face the shipwreck of *The Evorsio*, and felt a sharp pull in the center of his chest. The Tide Summoner was here. And it was calling to him.

Chapter Eighteen

THE SPINNING WHEEL

The *Evorsio* rested on the seabed like a tilted crown.

"Hurry up!" yelled Tara, from far, far away. She had stopped pushing the sea out. Their strip of seabed was growing narrower as the tide tightened its belt around them.

Fionn pressed a hand to his chest. Then, with their backs to the three black rocks, they hurried toward the shipwreck.

The shipwreck was more pristine than Fionn had been expecting—particularly compared to *La Juliana*. The body of it was barely submerged in the seabed, its hull tilted where broken masts had tipped it over. There were cannons strewn all around them, their slender bodies sticking out like posts. There were tattered black rags where billowing sails had once been. But the dark wood railings and intricate rig had been untouched by the ocean's curious mouths. The anchor was barely brushed with rust, its hefty tail wedged deep in the sand.

"Can you give me a boost?" said Shelby. "We need to go up on deck."

Fionn hoisted her onto his hands and then his shoulders as she pulled herself over the ship railings. He climbed on the head of the anchor and dragged himself up after her, his fingers closing around hers as she heaved him over the lip of the stern. A new smell nearly knocked him sideways. It was rotting fish and burned wood, ash and fire and metal. And something else. Something Fionn had never smelled before.

"*Oh*," said Shelby. "It's a *graveyard*."

The smell was death. And it was everywhere.

Fionn crunched a bone under his heel, swallowing his gasp before it sprang free. A skull stared up at him—the hollow remains of a merrow-chewed Soulstalker. They moved along quickly, picking their way over old bones and sunken wood, searching for the shell.

The sea inched closer. Tara's warnings rang out from the strand, where Sam was sitting down with his head tucked between his legs. It was just her and Bartley holding the tide now.

"Look," said Shelby, ducking under a broken mast and pointing toward the bow, where the ship's prow pierced the ocean's veil. They could see fish swimming around inside it—huge fins and curved bodies, their sleek scales glinting at them through the water.

The ship's wheel was spinning. A shiver of wind had followed them inside *The Evorsio* and was playing captain at the head of the vessel.

The wheel was knocking against something at its base.

It was a shell. It was covered in barnacles, laced with krill and coral, and stuffed with seaweed, but there was no mistaking the pearly exterior, or the gleaming gold rims.

They nearly tripped over themselves with the sudden burst of excitement, barely noticing the spray of saltwater on their cheeks as they thundered across the deck. Fionn's magic was in his throat, trying to scream. Trying to call out to the Tide Summoner.

Far away, Tara was screaming too.

Fionn tripped over a pile of bones and went down hard on his side, slamming into the deck with a painful "*Ooof!*"

Shelby vaulted over him, making a beeline for the shell. "It's okay. I got it!"

Fionn staggered to his feet just as Shelby yanked it

free. All around her, the ocean shook, like a giant block of blue jelly.

"Fionn!" She spun around, the shell glowing in her hand. The light encircled her fingers, and then her wrist, and then her arm, traveling all the way up her body like an electric current until her face was glowing too. She looked at him with wide eyes. "W-what's happening?"

Fionn stared at the shimmering shell. At her shimmering face. "Do you feel okay?"

Shelby swallowed. "I . . ."

Tara screamed.

The sea hiccuped.

"Shelby, *run*!" shouted Fionn as it rained down on them.

Shelby shoved the shell in her life jacket, and together they sprinted back across the deck, over ancient bones and gaping skulls, matching each other stride for stride. They flung themselves off the ship's railing and tumbled onto the seabed. The ocean poured over *The Evorsio*, gulping it back into its belly. It nipped at Fionn's heels as he leaped to his feet, his hand reaching for Shelby's as they bolted through the narrowing seabed, setting a course for the strand.

The ocean roared after them. The sea climbed up the black rocks and engulfed the Spanish shipwreck as they raced past it. Back on the beach, Bartley was on his knees.

Tara was the last one standing.

She was swaying on her feet.

The tide rushed in on either side of them, the pathway to shore no wider than the hallway at T*ír na n*Óg. Fionn slid behind Shelby, as the sea licked their elbows.

"We won't make it," Shelby panted. "We're too far."

Tara collapsed on the beach.

"Hold your breath!" yelled Fionn.

The sea careened over them, slammed their heads into the sand, and sluiced their legs out from under them. Fionn was lost in a cloud of froth and bubbles, his arms and legs flailing helplessly as the ocean buried him in an endless waterfall. He inhaled a lungful of saltwater and felt his chest closing. The life jacket pulled him up, up, up—until his head crested the surface. He threw his face back to the sky and vomited, gasping at the frigid air.

He spun in the water. "Shelby!"

He couldn't see her. Couldn't hear her. There was only the sound of his own panicked screams and the rattle of his cough in his ears. "Shelby!"

His insides grew white-hot, his magic flaring in every inch of him until he felt like he might explode from the heat of it.

The sea began to bubble.

"Shelby!" he yelled. "Shelby!"

Another mouthful of water poured out of him.

He hiccuped.

The waves hiccuped.

Shelby was thrown up from the sea.

She broke the surface in a tangle of hair and limbs, retching lungfuls of seawater as her life jacket suspended her. There was a gash along her forehead and a trail of blood covering one side of her face. "I hit a rock," she cried. "I got stuck!"

Her head began to loll, the blood dripping down her neck and soaking into her life jacket. The Tide Summoner sat snug against her chest.

Fionn swam toward her. "Hang on! I'm coming!"

"I'm so sleepy, Fionn."

"Stay awake, Shelby!" He pulled her into his chest and used his free hand to paddle them back to shore. It seemed impossibly far away. His sister was a blot on the sand, the others curled up on their sides beside her. "Keep talking to me."

"Too . . . tired."

"Tell me about the meerkats," he said, as the water lapped against his chin. "How did you get into the enclosure?"

Shelby smiled, her head collapsing against his shoulder. "Meerkats," she murmured. "Little tiny meerkats."

Come on, come on, come on.

He kicked his legs, groaning from the effort.

Please.

The wind picked up. The waves quietened as they moved through them. Fionn hoped she would be okay—that she would forgive him for wasting time in that stupid rock, for tripping over himself on the way to that shell. For dragging her with him in the first place.

Finally, after what seemed like an eternity, they were rolled out onto the sand. Shelby collapsed on top of him.

Bartley staggered over to them. "What happened?"

"She hit her head," said Fionn. "Get your phone. We need to call someone."

"My mom," said Bartley, patting his pockets in slow motion. "My mom's a doctor."

He took his phone out, blinking heavily as he raised it to his ear.

Fionn slipped his arms underneath Shelby's and dragged her up onto the beach. He wrestled the life jacket from her, stuffed the Tide Summoner in the waistband of his pants, and cleared the matted hair from her cheeks.

Sam crawled up the beach after them. He shrugged his coat off and pressed it against the cut on Shelby's forehead. "I'm sorry," he said blearily. "I fell asleep. I couldn't help it. I didn't know how exhausting it would be."

"It's not your fault. You did really well." Fionn grabbed

the empty backpack, stuffed his wet life jacket inside, and made a pillow for Shelby's head. "I wasted valuable time out there."

Tara groaned herself awake. Her eyelashes were crusted with sand, her right cheek bruising where she had gone down face first onto the beach. She dragged herself toward them. "Wha's happenin'?" she slurred.

"Come here! Quick!" said Fionn, waving her over. "I need to know what they do with concussions on that doctor show you love."

Tara peered over at Shelby. "Oh no," she said quietly. "I couldn't hold on any longer. I burned every single candle. I'm sorry."

Shelby's eyelashes fluttered. "Just hang on, Shelby," said Fionn. "Help is on the way."

They sat in a cluster, the Tide Summoner momentarily forgotten as they watched over their friend.

Finally, three figures appeared on the cliffs above.

"Mom!" Bartley waved his hands over his head as a tall woman in a dark navy suit stumbled down the rocks. Douglas Beasley followed after her, slipping and sliding his way into the cove. Elizabeth Beasley waited up on the cliffside, her silver hair streaming in the wind.

Shelby's mother landed on her like a butterfly. "It's okay, darling. Mommy's here." She removed Sam's coat, inspected the gash on her forehead. "Can you open your eyes for me, Shelby?"

Douglas hovered over her shoulder, his beady eyes trained on Bartley. "How did this happen?" he demanded. "Haven't I told you to be careful near those bloody rocks?"

"We were—"

"Weren't you watching your sister?" Douglas interrupted. "Look how hurt she is. There's enough danger on these shores without adding your idiocy to the list! When your father gets down here, he'll clip your ear!"

"I—I know. But we had to get the Tide Summoner . . ."

"That stupid shell again," said Douglas, shaking his head. "For goodness' *sake*."

"She hit her head." Bartley raked a hand through his hair. It was a mess now, matted with gel and mussed with sand. "It's not my fault."

Bartley's mother sat back, her mouth relaxing. Her hooded eyes were light brown and marked at their corners with crow's feet. They were warmer than Fionn was expecting. "She's all right, Douglas. She'll need some stitches and supervision. Let's get her home."

Shelby was awake, and staring at them like they had all sprouted several extra heads. "What's all the fuss about?"

"Douglas, help me get her up. She needs to get out of this cove and into the warmth."

"I'm fine," said Shelby, trying to sit up. She winced. "*Ouch.*"

"What on earth happened down here?" Shelby's mother was just now registering Tara, who was half slumped against a rock, Sam caught mid-yawn, and finally Bartley, whose eyes were so red it looked as though he hadn't slept in a week. He was so unusually quiet now, Fionn wondered if he might have a concussion.

"The Storm Keeper looks fine to me," said Douglas, turning on Fionn. "Whatever this mess was, you shouldn't have endangered my niece. Don't we have enough to worry about today?"

"I'm sorry," said Fionn quietly. "It was an accident."

"Go home," said Douglas. "You'll have a lot to answer for later. And you could do with a bath. You smell like a decomposing seal."

"H*a*," said Bartley weakly.

Fionn gathered up Sam and Tara, dragging them along behind him as they left the Beasleys to take Shelby.

On the top of the cliff, Elizabeth skewered them with her burning glare. If she'd hated Fionn before, then she *despised* him now. "I hope you have something very clever up your sleeve for our meeting later, Keeper," she said darkly. "For our sake *and yours.*"

Fionn held his tongue this time, but he could feel her eyes boring into his back as they slunk away from her.

"Nosy old woman," muttered Sam.

"Just hurry up," said Tara, leaning heavily on him. "We need to get home."

Fionn pulled the Tide Summoner from his waistband. The gold rims winked at him beneath a crust of barnacles. He pulled a mound of seaweed from its mouth, dropping the strands in his wake.

"What now?" asked Sam, perking up a little.

Fionn traced the rim. "We'll blow it on the strand at sundown, when Ivan has his entire army out on the beach looking for me," he said, twisting the shell in his hands. "That way, we can summon our own army. And they'll rip his to shreds in less than five minutes."

"It's about time we turned the tide in our favor," said Tara approvingly.

"Yeah," said Fionn, a cautious smile curling on his lips. "It is."

Chapter Nineteen

THE LAUGHING THIEF

When they returned to the headland, Fionn slipped the end of his grandfather's candle from his pocket. "I'm going to burn this to sneak back inside."

"There's no one there," said Sam, who had stalked ahead, to where the little cottage edged into view. "The garden's empty."

Fionn and Tara exchanged a suspicious glance.

"What do you mean?" asked Tara as she hurried to Sam's side. "*Oh*."

The garden at *Tír na nÓg* was indeed curiously absent of Soulstalkers, the deserted headland now smooth and glassy with a fresh layer of frost. It covered the cottage in a glistening blanket, trickling from the rooftop in dainty icicles. The scene was as pretty as a watercolor painting. In another time, Fionn might have hovered a moment longer, even taken a photo of it with his phone, if it weren't for the ravens perched on the chimney, or the front door blown wide open.

"*Fionn*," said Tara uneasily.

Sam ducked as a raven launched off the roof and swooped at his head, its hooked beak snapping at his ears. "Get off!"

Tara slapped another one away as they raced across the headland and through the open gate.

Ivan met them in the doorway. "Hello, children."

Fionn skidded to a stop. Tara slammed into his shoulder, and the candle stub tumbled from his grasp. "*Ooof!*"

"Found him!" Ivan called over his shoulder, his eyes never leaving Fionn's. "Where *have* you been, Storm Keeper? And how on *earth* did you manage to slip past so many of us?"

Tara turned on Sam and shoved him out the gate. "Run!" she told him. "Get help!"

Sam ran and the birds followed, shrieking after him like banshees.

Ivan removed a candle from behind his back and dangled it before them. "I suppose this must be your little secret. I can practically taste the magic." With his grin fixed beneath his bright bushy beard, he snapped the candle with a *crack!* "It makes me *sick*."

Tara gasped.

Ivan threw the broken candle over their heads and out onto the headland. "I suppose you won't be needing them anymore."

Inside the cottage, Fionn's mother screamed.

Tara darted around Fionn and threw herself at Ivan. "*Move!*"

"Tara! Don't!" shouted Fionn.

Ivan batted her away. She went flying into a rosebush, her hands coming to her face as the thorns jabbed at her skin.

Ivan stalked toward Fionn. "How about you just come with me now?" he said, as a chorus of shouts rang out from inside the cottage. "Save the islanders the shame of betraying you. Save your family the trouble of dying for you."

"How about you get your zombie Soulstalkers out of my house and off my island?" Fionn backed away from Ivan. He pictured himself pushing off the ground and flying into the sky. Ripping a tree from the earth and skewering Ivan's heart. Scooping him up in the wind and throwing him over the cliffs. In those precious few seconds, he imagined some thousand-and-one things he would do, though none of them came to pass. "I'm not going *anywhere* with you."

"You're out of time, Storm Keeper. Leaders make armies, not wax. Even your islanders have lost faith in you." He swept his hand around at the glassy planes of winter, at the island dying underneath his feet. "You can't even use your own magic."

"W-what?" Fionn spluttered. "Of course I can."

Ivan laughed. "Then why are your family killing themselves to protect you right now? If you weren't so useless you'd fight back, but you haven't made a single attempt to hurt me, despite the sound of your own mother's screams behind me."

"If I'm so powerless, come and get me." Fionn held Ivan's gaze—the Soulstalker's eyes like dark tunnels in his narrow face—as his sister untangled herself from the rosebush and crept inside the cottage. "Shouldn't it be easy for you?"

Ivan marched toward him. "All these months of tireless *searching* for my people, through endless winters and lost villages, forgotten towns and faraway countries, have led me back here, to *this* moment, and you really think I won't finish what I started? She will rise when the Storm Keeper bleeds for her. You're my final puzzle piece, boy."

Fionn moved his hands behind his back. "What if I don't *feel* like bleeding for you?"

"Then I'll cut down every man, woman, and child on this little island, until you do *feel* like it," he said nonchalantly. "Don't you understand the power of my influence? Don't you see how every single Soulstalker does *exactly* what I say?"

"I was wondering about that," said Fionn, deftly reaching under his coat. "Why *do* all the other Soulstalkers seem to listen to *you*?"

"Because Morrigan *speaks* to me," said Ivan. "She speaks *through* me."

Moving as little as possible, Fionn worked the shell free from his waistband. "So you're her favorite. It must be slim pickings."

"Not quite." Ivan's smile was saccharine, stretched wide with the closeness of a secret. "I'm her brother."

There was a beat of pure silence. The world stopped turning. Even the wind seemed to pause and listen.

Fionn's fingers lost their purchase. "Her *brother*?" He could barely say the word.

"Oh yes." Ivan tilted his head. "Morrigan murdered my father—he was always a threat to her, you see." Behind him, a scream rose up and a Soulstalker was hurled out of the cottage. She landed in a heap on the garden path, clutching her head in her hands. "But my brothers and I, we were *useful*. We had our father's power but not his . . . *ambition*. Our magic could be tamed."

"There are *more* of you?" said Fionn.

The grass crunched under Ivan's footsteps.

"Your legends are wrong, Keeper. Morrigan killed every single magic-born human on her way to Dagda. Save for *three*. She left us alive, but bound us to her. *We* led her army with more cunning and bloodthirstiness than the world had ever seen. *We* were the reason for her success. The Three Stags, the old world called us. The Brutal, the Cunning, and the Silent." Another step. "We were the pyramid upon which she ruled. And we will be so again. When my sister is raised, our full strength will be returned to us once more. Our magic finally restored to our veins."

Fionn was nearing the edge of the headland. The water roared far below, like it was trying to tell him something. "Black point rock," he gasped. With sudden, sickening clarity, he understood what those sea shards really were. "You broke out of your tomb."

Ivan laughed. "It never sealed me in."

Another scream from across the headland. *Tara*. There was no sign of her in the garden, just the dark whip of her ponytail as she leaped past the open door, a candle burning in her fist. Then another Soulstalker tumbled through the air.

Fionn held Ivan's stare, keeping a firm grip on his attention. "But *how*?"

"Aldric, Bredon, and I belonged to the earth, just as Morrigan did—tied to her by our blood, we shared the same fate, but when the island reached out to claim us, I was quick," he said, smiling at his own ingenuity. "*Cunning*. I escaped." He looked past Fionn to the wild Atlantic Ocean, and Fionn knew what he was picturing in his mind: those three black shards tucked around the back of the island. His brothers, waiting to be freed.

Fionn shuddered at the thought of it. There wasn't a second to waste now—even if Ivan threw him off this cliff and he plummeted to a watery death, he owed it to the island to make sure those brothers never saw the light of day. That Morrigan was never freed from that Sea Cave.

"You abandoned your family," said Fionn, holding the Tide Summoner tight behind his back.

Ivan's left eye twitched. "I came back for them."

"Oh, I know," said Fionn, leading him farther down the headland. "I *saw* you all those years ago, quivering on the deck of *The Evorsio*. I watched my ancestor destroy your fleet with his bare hands, and then I watched you scrabbling up the mast, like a beetle. Climbing for your life."

Ivan's smile faltered.

"You were so *afraid* back then," Fionn went on. "But the merrows are quite terrifying, aren't they? They can eat an entire Soulstalker in one bite. I know because I've seen it. But then again, so have you."

"You weren't there," said Ivan, a note of uncertainty creeping into his voice.

"I've been everywhere," said Fionn. "Didn't you know that?"

There was another cry from inside the cottage. This time the front window shattered and a Soulstalker's face appeared in the frame, the broken glass cutting lines on his cheeks. There were five more piled in the front garden.

"Shouldn't you go and check on that?" said Fionn.

Ivan lunged at him.

Fionn jumped backward, teetering on the edge of the headland, as he raised the Tide Summoner to his lips.

Ivan grappled at thin air. "NO!"

Fionn blew into the shell.

One heartbeat . . . five heartbeats . . .

Nothing.

Ivan's lip curled.

Fionn blew again, his cheeks swelling as he pushed his breath through the mouthpiece. He felt it disappear into the shell, but no noise came, no eerie echo hanging in the air.

Fionn shook the last vestiges of seaweed from it, desperation flooding his body as he blew again. Harder this time. He could feel Dagda's magic throbbing inside the shell, felt the same magic wide awake in his chest. Watching. Waiting.

No sound.

Nothing.

Ivan laughed. "Quick like your ancestor, but not as smart. It's not bound to you, is it, Keeper?"

Fionn stared at the shell.

Lay worthy hands upon the shell,

And breath becomes the ocean's knell.

The merrow had told him, but he hadn't listened. Not properly. The hands that found it were certainly worthy, but they hadn't been his.

The bond that takes a touch to make

Will not before a lifetime break.

The Tide Summoner wasn't tied to him.

It was tied to Shelby.

"I could find a use for it though." Ivan leaped at Fionn. The shell tumbled from his grasp as the Soulstalker grabbed him by the neck, dangling him over the roiling ocean. There was an awful stretch of nothingness—the wind roaring in Fionn's ears, the sea air rippling up his back.

Ivan whipped him around by his collar and flung him across the headland. He landed with a hard thud, rolling over three times before coming to a stop nose first in the dirt. "*Ooomph.*"

Ivan twirled the Tide Summoner in his hands. "Perhaps we'll see what our queen can do with Dagda's craftwork. Perhaps she won't need *you* at all."

"Give me that!"

Ivan slammed his foot down on his wrist. "Such powerful ancient magic, ripe for the taking," he said, with giddy amusement. "For the *twisting*. And what better night than the solstice to turn it dark?"

Fionn hadn't stopped to consider what the Tide Summoner would do in the wrong hands. "Thief," he hissed. "That belongs to Dagda!"

"Is he here to claim it?" Ivan lifted the shell above his head and brought it crashing down like a hammer. Fionn rolled over, just in time to see it take a clump out of the frosty earth.

There was an almighty screech. Another Soulstalker pinwheeled through the air. Fionn's grandfather appeared in the doorway, a candle burning in one hand, his other raised above him. ". . . AND STAY OUT!"

Fionn leaped to his feet, ducking, as his grandfather flung a ball of wind at Ivan, hitting him square between the eyes.

"Run, lad! Hurry!"

Fionn sprinted back up the headland, vaulted over the pile of groaning Soulstalkers, and skidded down the garden path. Inside, the cottage was in disarray, candles toppled from their perches and rolling around the wooden floors. So many had been split in two—the wax crushed along the floorboards, their wicks ripped out like innards.

The Christmas tree had been bashed in and the kitchen table lay toppled on its side. The candle on the mantelpiece pushed its dying flame into the chaos, but Fionn's grandfather was already slumping against the doorframe. The half-used candle was limp in his hand, exertion reddening his cheeks. Tara was doubled over on the floor, retching. There were fresh cuts across her face and thorns tangled in her hair. Her hands were stained with different-colored wax. "I can't do any more magic, Fionny," she heaved. "I'm so tired, I can barely see."

Ivan marched into the garden. He was the only Soulstalker still standing, but he paid no heed to the others as he passed them.

Fionn's mother filled up the doorway, like a specter. "Leave my family *alone*, you lousy little creep!" With a candle in her left hand and her free palm facing out, she ripped a rosebush clean out of the earth and sent it spiraling at Ivan.

He leaped backward, bringing his hands to his face.

Fionn's grandfather wheezed a chuckle. "Nice one, Evie."

Fionn's mother gritted her teeth as she grappled with another rosebush. The branches creaked and then went limp, their roots dug tightly in the frosty earth. She staggered backward, the candle falling from her fist.

"Let me guess," said Ivan, as he sauntered toward her. "Over your dead body, right?"

Fionn charged through the doorway and ran at Ivan. They went down hard on the grass, kicking and punching each other. Fionn tasted blood on his tongue and felt himself fill up with it. His teeth were chattering in his mouth, his magic thrumming hot inside his veins. He arched his back and tried to kick out at Ivan as he tightened his grip on Fionn's throat.

The ground thumped, the island's heartbeat as fast as his own. The earth vaulted upward, like something was trying to burst out. Ivan was thrown skyward. He landed on his pile of Soulstalkers with a bone-cracking thud. He sat up, bleary-eyed, the Tide Summoner clutched to his chest.

The earth thumped as Fionn stalked toward him. Ivan struggled to his feet and backed away from Fionn, beckoning to his fallen comrades. "Get up, you fools. *Move! Quick!*"

There was fear clouding the Soulstalkers' eyes, not of Fionn but of what was coming up the headland behind him. Fionn glanced over his shoulder to find a small crowd marching up the hill. Sam was leading the way, swinging his flute like a battle-ax. Behind him, his father was carrying his illegal hunting rifle, and his mother was spinning what looked like a metal curtain pole. Niall Cannon had come too, carrying a battered hurling stick. Tom Rowan followed up the rear with his pitchfork.

It was by no means an army.

But it was enough to chase the worn-out Soulstalkers away.

They stumbled over each other in retreat. Ivan glared at Fionn over his shoulder, angry spittle foaming in his beard. "When the sun sets, this island is mine, Storm Keeper!"

With the Tide Summoner held hostage in his grasp, he turned on his heel and bolted.

Chapter Twenty

THE END OF TIME

The wind carried the dead rosebushes over the cliff and tossed them into the sea. In their absence, the winter sun streamed in through the broken windows at *Tír na nÓg*, banishing the shadows from its corners. While his family slept, Fionn and the other islanders plucked the broken candles from the floor. The Soulstalkers had destroyed most of them, cracked their spines and crushed the wax. They tidied the casualties away; old storms and shattered sunsets, falling skies and weeping rainbows—irretrievably broken. Gone forever now.

"There's less than four hundred left," said Sam, who had set about counting them in the sitting room. "Three hundred and eighty-seven, to be exact."

Niall, who was fixing the Christmas tree, stuck his head out from between the branches. "That's over one hundred shy of the island's population."

"Not if you don't include the non-descendants. Not to mention the elderly and the young," said Sam's mother, who had set her curtain pole aside to wipe down the walls, which were marred by bloody fingerprints and dark burn marks. "There'll be enough for those who can use them."

"*Just* enough," heaved Sam's father, as he and Tom hoisted the kitchen table right-side up.

Fionn sighed. It would be enough for one last stand.

Which might not be enough at all.

With Niall's help, he culled the snapped branches on the Christmas tree and mended the string of blinking lights. He cleared the broken baubles from its feet and rearranged those that had rolled away in the scuffle.

Tom removed the headless Santa Claus from the hallway, dragged it outside, and wedged it in the garden shed, while Sam arranged the salvaged candles in a sprawling pile on the couch.

Little by little, they erased the Soulstalkers from *Tír na nÓg*. But Fionn couldn't erase the memory of the Tide Summoner carted off in Ivan's greedy hands, their greatest weapon come and gone in the same morning. What a fool he'd been—arrogant and thoughtless and impetuous, a poor imitation of Hughie Rua. He should have been more careful. He should have protected Shelby in that ocean. He should never have become Storm Keeper in the first place.

What was the island *thinking*?

When the others had gone, with the promise of meeting again shortly in the school hall, and the cottage had been restored to a glimmer of its former self, Fionn resettled the Storm Keeper ornament atop the tree. It twirled slowly, watching him with its little hollow eyes.

"I'm sorry," he said quietly. "I know I'm useless."

The Keeper only twirled, turning its gaze to the world outside.

Fionn wandered into the kitchen and collapsed in a chair. The island meeting would soon be upon them, and he had nothing to show for it. He would have to tell all the islanders the truth—that the Tide Summoner was lost, and their supply of candles hopelessly dwindled. Who would stand with him now?

After a while, Fionn's grandfather stirred from his nap and wandered into the kitchen. He sat on the other side of the table, drumming a steady rhythm against the splintered wood while Fionn cataloged the cuts and bruises on his face. The silence stretched out, the sound of crashing waves filtering through the broken window and settling around them until it felt like they were bobbing together on an endless ocean.

It was Fionn who broke the silence. "Ivan is Morrigan's brother."

His grandfather *hmm*'d. "Well, that explains the sense of entitlement."

"There are two more brothers buried in Black Point Rock," added Fionn. "He was more than happy to tell me about them."

"Well," said his grandfather distantly. "Who doesn't love a good reveal?"

"Aren't you *scared*?" Fionn blinked at him. "Ivan has the Tide Summoner and *two brothers* in his back pocket. Do you realize what this means? What we're facing now?"

His grandfather sighed. "There is a more pressing matter than Morrigan's family reunion, I'm afraid." He rolled his shoulders back, took a deep breath, and spoke the words Fionn had been dreading all winter. "My candle has almost run out." He gestured through the archway into the sitting room, where a flame flickered weakly from the glass trough on the mantelpiece. "I would like you to help me remake it into something less . . . unwieldy."

Fionn stared through the archway at the candle, as his world began to spin. There was an aching fullness gathering in the base of his throat. A twin ache behind his eyes.

"I'd like to do it now, if we can," said his grandfather gently. "Is that all right?"

"Fine," said Fionn, in a hollow voice. "Let's get it over with, then."

They crossed into the little sitting room, stood at either end of the mantelpiece, and lifted the candle. The trough was heavy—weighted not by the meager puddle of wax inside but the glass that bordered it. They carried it across the sitting room and down the little hallway, where Fionn's grandfather pushed through the back door. They settled it on the workbench and stood over the flame.

The wax made a thin coat of blue paint on the glass bottom, most of it turned to liquid by the candle's heat. Fionn imagined tipping over the edge of the trough and pouring himself in, using his blood and his magic and his heart and his soul to squeeze more time from this place. More impossibility.

"There's so little of it left," he said. "I could have sworn there was almost double this last night."

His grandfather rummaged underneath the workbench and set a new candle mold between them. "Time is funny here," he said, rolling the stalk of a new wick between his fingers. "It crawls. It flies. There's no predicting it."

"Time is cruel here," said Fionn bitterly.

His grandfather flicked the silver disc until it *ping*ed.

Then he stuck it to the bottom of the mold. "This candle has been an impossible, imperfect gift. And that's how we must look at it."

Fionn sat down and pressed his fists against his eyes. "But *why* can't we just be angry? Doesn't that feel much more satisfying?"

"Because gratitude for what we have been gifted is the antidote to the grief we feel when we must give it back." His grandfather unfurled the burner flame from underneath the workbench and turned it on. "Don't you think that would make an excellent fridge magnet?"

"No," said Fionn sulkily.

His grandfather chuckled. "Well, in any case, we are not yet out of time." He tapped the side of the trough, his fingernails *click-clack*ing along the glass. "I bled enough to make this candle, and believe me when I tell you, lad, I intend to use every last drop of it."

Fionn folded his hands on the bench. There was a robin perched on the garden shed, chirping happily at them. He glared at it. "Shut up."

The robin puffed its little red breast up and trilled louder.

"Ugh."

"Shush," said his grandfather. "Don't you know they spy for Santa?"

Fionn rolled his eyes.

"Are you ready then, lad?" he said more seriously.

"Yeah. I'm ready."

"Quick as you can. Let's go." His grandfather leaned over the trough and blew the candle out.

The workbench shook. A thin curl of smoke rose up into the sky, and Fionn swore the breeze stopped jostling the bare branches.

His grandfather slumped on the stool. "What . . . what time is it?"

"It's about eleven thirty." Fionn got to his feet. "Can you help me lift this, please? I need to heat the rest of the wax in the trough."

His grandfather knitted his brows together. "Why?"

"We're making a new candle," said Fionn.

Fionn's grandfather got to his feet and lifted the other end of the trough. "It's awful heavy, Cormac. Can't you just melt new wax?"

"This is special wax," said Fionn. "Just hold it steady, please. It will be done soon."

They suspended the trough above the burner, moving it back and forth above the blue flame until the wax inside turned runny and smooth.

"What are we doing?" His grandfather peered into the trough. "What is all this?"

“We’re making a new candle,” said Fionn. “A smaller one.”

“Where’s your mother? I should probably get down to the boats before lunch.”

“It won’t be lunch for a while yet. We’re almost finished now.”

“What time is it?”

“About eleven thirty.”

“Is your mother inside?”

“I’m not sure,” said Fionn. “Can you hold your side up, while I tip the wax into the new mold?”

His grandfather frowned. “I should check on the boats. I want to be back in time for lunch.”

Fionn pulled the used wick from the glass bottom and set it aside. Then he tilted the trough and carefully poured the remaining wax into the new mold, making sure he saved every single drop. It was no bigger than a pint glass, the wick white as winter snow.

Then the trough was empty. They set it down. A small part of Fionn wanted to smash it into pieces. He rotated the new mold as the wax dried inside it.

Fionn’s grandfather collapsed onto his stool. “What is that?”

“It’s time,” said Fionn quietly. “The end of time.”

“Time,” his grandfather repeated on a breath.

The wax shimmered, the faintest scent of summer

seas rising from it, the final minutes of a blazing sunset. His grandfather sniffed. "Oh," he said, drawing back. He looked at Fionn, the crevices in his forehead deepening. "Cormac?" he said uncertainly.

Fionn held a breath.

"No." His grandfather shook his head. "But Cormac is dead." He thumped his chest. "My poor boy. My boy is dead."

Fionn prized the new candle from the mold. "Hang on."

"And Winnie," said his grandfather, his hands coming to his face. "Oh, my darling Winnie. My Winnie has left me."

Fionn lit the new candle with shaking fingers. The flame climbed, pouring the ocean into the garden and sprinkling the blue back into his grandfather's eyes.

Fionn set it down between them.

Come on, come on, come on.

His grandfather groaned. "I don't . . ." He trailed off. "I'm not sure what . . . I'm confused."

"I know," said Fionn. "It's okay. I promise."

"I'm afraid," he whispered.

Fionn squeezed his eyes shut. "I know you are, Grandad."

I'm afraid too.

He opened his eyes and glared at the candle. He couldn't tell what he wanted more—to stretch its magic out and live inside it, not moving forward, not moving at all. Or to speed time up, so the pain could come all at once and drown him in a waterfall.

His grandfather touched his fingers against the wax. "Fionn," he sighed. "*Fionn*."

Fionn nodded. "Yeah. Fionn."

His grandfather wiped the tears from his cheeks. "You did it, lad. Well done. It looks perfectly fine, doesn't it?"

The candle looked perfectly small.

"I can't believe that's all that's left," he said, lifting it to inspect it. "After all this time."

"At least it's done," said Fionn, shoving his stool away from the table, from this moment, and from everything it meant for his family.

"Fionn," his grandfather called after him. "Wait."

Fionn froze with his hand against the back door.

"There's one more thing . . ."

Fionn turned on the heel of his shoe. "What . . . one thing?"

His grandfather was tracing the lip of the empty trough.

Fionn drifted back to the bench. "Whatever it is, just say it."

His grandfather pushed his spectacles up his nose and looked him straight in the eyes. "I made this candle with my blood and my magic, Fionn. I'm sure you can see how it was almost an impossibility. But I made a plea to the island to give me more *time*. Just a little more time."

Fionn felt like he was standing on the edge of a cliff, and any second, his grandfather was going to push him over it.

"Because you see, lad, you were a little late getting here," he went on. "And, well, I was losing bits and pieces of myself while I waited." His smile was faint. "It was important I was here when you arrived, so that I could *help* you in whatever way you needed me to . . ."

"What do you mean I was 'late'?" said Fionn.

His grandfather glanced at the cottage, the ghost of a thought passing over his face. "I suppose that doesn't matter much now, lad. You came in the end."

In the end.

Fionn lowered himself to the workbench, his heart-beat pounding in his ears.

"The island answered my plea," his grandfather went on. "It took my blood and my magic and it mixed them together to give me more time. Time with *you*. However . . ."

"No," said Fionn, hearing it before he said it. "Please don't."

"I made the bargain with my mind *and* my body." He glanced at the candle. "The strength from one side of me to feed the other. Do you understand what I'm trying to say?"

Fionn swallowed. The truth had grown jagged teeth; it gnawed at him in the silence, tearing strips from his heart. "Please don't say it," he whispered.

"When the wax melts, my memories will fade for good. And my life will follow soon after." He stared at Fionn blankly, his mouth set into a hard line. It was as if he had been preparing for this moment his entire life, navigating the tightrope of his own impending doom with unnerving composure. "So you see, Fionn, it will soon be time for me to go. For good. The timing, I admit, is less than ideal."

Fionn felt like he had swallowed a balloon. It burst open in his chest. "You're going to leave me," he sobbed, and his whole body shook. "I'll be all alone again."

"Oh, Fionn." His grandfather leaned across the workbench and took his hand in his. "You will be with your mother and Tara and Shelby and Sam. And I will be with Winnie and Cormac. What could be more wonderful than that?"

"If you were *with me*," said Fionn, with a burst of wet anger. "If you *stayed* with me!"

"But I'll *always* be with you, Fionn, no matter *where* I am. Don't you believe that?"

Fionn eyed the candle. He hated the flame for its greediness, hated the wax for its paltriness. He curled his arms around his stomach. “I’m not ready,” said Fionn. “I don’t want to say goodbye yet.”

“Then we’ll say ‘see you later,’ ” his grandfather said, shedding his melancholy as easily as a raincoat. “We mustn’t be sad.”

It was like telling the sun not to shine or night not to fall. It was Fionn’s condition—a pendulum that swung ceaselessly, from fear to pain and pain to fear. “All I am is sad.”

His grandfather lifted the candle from the workbench. “There is a time to weep, lad, but it is not this day,” he said in a steady voice. “We have work to do and plans to hatch, and, I’m afraid to say, there’s no time to be sad about any of it right now. You’ll have to wait. Do you see this beautiful hunk of wax?” He rotated the candle. “This is a gift and we’re going to *use* it. Time will not end when I do. The wind will not stop blowing and the world will not stop turning. The sun will set and the moon will rise. You will still have work to do, and places to go, and people to lead, and people to love. It is up to us to fight for that right. It is up to us to reach out and grab that possibility before it’s taken away from us for good.”

“What if I had never come here, Grandad? What if I had never woken her up?”

His grandfather looked past him. “It’s hard to wonder about roads not taken, Fionn, but it is my belief that we couldn't have stopped this by avoiding it. The island was weakening without you. I could feel it in my own veins, the waning of my magic. It would have left us, eventually, and then there would have been only darkness breathing through the earth. Morrigan was always going to wake up, Fionn."

"And now she has the Tide Summoner," said Fionn angrily. "A big hunk of Dagda's magic."

"And we have our people," said his grandfather. "There is power in numbers."

"But what can I offer them?" Fionn stared at his hands, the faint blue lines underneath his skin. "I can't even understand my own magic. Sometimes I can feel it fizzing underneath my skin. It does things—little things—without me telling it to." He thought of Hughie Rua's sinking boat, of Shelby thrown up from the sea. "Today in the garden, it was like the *earth* was trying to help me. Quaking and thumping until it threw Ivan off me, and then"—he wiggled his fingers—"it faded again. Like it always does. Sometimes it feels like my magic is on my side, and it knows what I need. And then other times . . ." He closed his eyes and tried to feel for a whisper of warmth inside himself, but there was nothing. "Other times, it feels as if it's not there at all."

"I have been grappling with the peculiarity of this,

Fionn," admitted his grandfather. "It seems the less you think about your magic, the better it works. Perhaps it's not linked to your mind, but to something else entirely." He frowned.

"But *why*?" asked Fionn. "I don't understand why I'm different to every other Storm Keeper, *ever*."

"Not yet, you don't. But sometimes we must trust in the things we don't yet know," said his grandfather placidly. "Another fridge magnet, no?"

"No," said Fionn flatly.

His grandfather chuckled. "What time is it, lad?"

Fionn pulled out his phone. "It's almost noon."

"Good." He sprang to his feet. "The day is bright. The sun is high. We are not yet out of time. We'd better wake your sister and your mother," he said, marching back into the cottage, the last remnants of himself held tight inside his fist. "We have a very important meeting to get to."

Fionn stared after him. "What do you mean, *we*?"

His grandfather waggled the candle above his head. "This is the silver lining, Fionn. Take a good look at it. Our new candle is portable, and that means I am too."

Chapter Twenty-One

THE LOST VISION

The school hall was packed to the rafters. The events of this morning had spread quickly, onlookers carrying word of Ivan's attack on *Tír na nÓg* to the farthest corners of Arranmore, where it leaped from house to house like wildfire.

Fionn shuffled to the front of the crowd with his grandfather beside him; Storm Keepers—past and present—come to perform their final duty before time splintered them apart for good. Tara and his mother marched after them, their coat pockets stuffed with candles, the rest of them piled in heavy carrier bags at their sides. They sat in the front row, where Sam and his family were wedged between a sea of other Pattons. Douglas

Beasley was several rows back, his thick head and broad shoulders setting him apart from a set of smaller, more diminutive Beasleys. A slightly dazed Shelby sat beside him with her father, a thinner, paler version of Douglas, who was, mercifully, mustache-free.

She waved at Fionn, pointing proudly at the new square bandage on her forehead. "Ten stitches," she mouthed.

Fionn tried to smile but he couldn't stop the shame heating his cheeks. He had taken and lost Shelby's Tide Summoner in a single hour, and now they had nothing to show for their perilous journey but the scar on her forehead.

After what seemed like an age, Fionn reached the top of the hall, where he hovered under the watchful gaze of five hundred faces, some pale with fear, others pinched with hostility. Elizabeth had seated herself two rows from the front, her hawklike eyes boring into him with such force, he felt it in the pit of his stomach. He looked past her, to the Cannons, who waved at him encouragingly.

Come on. Just get on with it.

"Thank you all for coming." Fionn's voice echoed back at him from the rafters. He was conscious of the clock on the wall, the clock screaming in his head. *Tick-tock, tick-tock.* "I wish I had better news for you, but there's no point in sugarcoating the truth now," he said, relaying the speech he had rehearsed with his grandfather. "As you know, Morrigan will rise again tonight if we don't do something to stop her. Ivan's promise that he will spare you if you hand me over is a lie. He is Morrigan's brother, and the leader of her army. All he cares about is restoring her to power once more. Today I went on a secret mission to recover the lost Tide Summoner, a shell that will call the merrows to our aid. But when I got home, Ivan was there. He stole it from me."

Someone at the back of the hall gasped.

"Ivan also destroyed a lot of the candles. Our supply of magical weapons has been drastically reduced." He took a deep breath, tears prickling behind his eyes when he said, "And I'm sorry. I'm really sorry for letting you all down."

Silence then. Horrible, swelling, soul-crushing silence.

"But the candles were our defense," said Una Patton, from the front row. "We've been practicing so hard with them. We were *good*."

"Some of us were *brilliant*," said Douglas Beasley angrily.

"There are still some left," said Fionn, with as much confidence as he could muster. "And I have a plan for them. But I need your help . . ."

Wide eyes and bated breath. A nebula of nervous energy, hanging on his every word.

"Well, get on with it then," said Douglas.

"Ivan has been keeping his Soulstalkers down in the Sea Cave. That's where he's taken the Tide Summoner. There's only one course of action left now . . . I want us to use the remaining candles to attack the Sea Cave together before nightfall."

The silence shattered, an aria of whispers suddenly filling up the hall. The island blew a breeze in through the windows, rattled chair legs and purse straps. A baby started crying somewhere at the back of the hall. One of the Cannon twins screeched, Alva diving into the aisle to yank him back onto her lap.

Elizabeth Beasley's voice rose above the fray. "You can't *possibly* expect us all to go down into that terrible, cursed place and risk our lives like that. To stand against an enemy who already outnumber us. We know exactly what they're capable of." She pressed a hand to her collarbone. "*Surely* there's a better way?"

"Not with what we have left," said Fionn. "We have to get the Tide Summoner back before sunset or Ivan will twist its magic and destroy it forever."

"Or we could just hand you over, in exchange for our safety?" said Douglas Beasley.

Shelby turned to glare at him. "How could you even *suggest* such a thing, Uncle Douglas?"

"Come on now, Doug," said Niall. "Be reasonable."

"I'm only saying what we're all thinking." Douglas looked around, searching the sea of frightened faces. "The odds have changed—*drastically*, it appears. Our defenses have dwindled. We need to find a new solution to this mess."

"If you hand me over, Morrigan will be back before dawn," said Fionn. "It won't be the end of the island's suffering . . . it will only be the beginning."

"Well, that sounds like something you *would* say," muttered Douglas.

"So why don't we just leave then?" said Juliana Aguero. "All of us together. *Today*."

"How are we supposed to do that?" said Shelby. "They've destroyed all our boats!"

"We can try to call the coastguards," suggested Donal. "Request a mass evacuation. It will be dangerous, especially with Ivan lurking on the island. We'd need to make at least ten trips, but we might be able to pull it off, if we're quick and quiet."

Murmurs rippled through the hall.

"That won't stop them," said Fionn, shaking his head. "The Soulstalkers are *awake*. They remember who they are. Why they're here. They'll raise Morrigan one way or another. Then they'll spread their power to the mainland, and before we know it the whole country will be dead or enslaved." He clenched his fists by his sides. "There *is* another way. We can stay and fight. If we can get the Tide Summoner back, we can stop this battle before it even begins and defeat the Soulstalkers once and for all. We can save the world, together, like Dagda always intended."

A horrible laugh filled the room, like the high-pitched titter of a cruel bird. "Well, I for one am not going to risk my life because of your continued incompetence, *Storm Keeper*," said Elizabeth, standing up.

"Spoken like a true Beasley, Elizabeth," said Fionn's mother.

"And you wonder why you haven't had a Storm Keeper in eight generations," added Sam's father.

"So, you all intend to die for this *foolish* plan?" said Elizabeth viciously. "For this *foolish* boy."

Fionn's grandfather shot up from his seat. "My grandson is no fool, Betty."

Elizabeth raised a spindly finger. "And you're even worse for allowing it, Malachy. What *on earth* has possessed you to back this ridiculous idea?"

"My *son*," said Fionn's grandfather. He raised the candle in his right hand, and Fionn felt the heat of his anger, as if it was a real furnace burning around him. "My *only son*, Cormac, died so that Fionn would live to save these shores from terrible darkness." His words came down like the crack of a whip. "I know because I saw it in the Whispering Tree when I was fifteen years old. If we don't strike now, Morrigan will kill us all."

"But how can we take your word for it, Malachy? I saw you only days ago outside your house and you had no idea who I was." Elizabeth turned slowly, like a figurine in a music box, so that the islanders could look at her smug face. "In fact, I would bet that half the time, you don't even know your own self."

There was an awkward clearing of throats, a shuffling of chair legs. Averted gazes.

Elizabeth narrowed her eyes. "Do you deny it?"

"No," he said simply. "I don't deny it."

"Well, that's it then." Elizabeth swatted his words away. "Our only remaining witness to the importance of the boy's plan is completely unreliable."

Fionn's mother stood up, her chair screeching in the bated silence.

"My husband, Cormac, saw Morrigan and Fionn in the Whispering Tree three months before he drowned."

Fionn reeled backward. "What?"

His grandfather turned his head sharply.

Tara stared up at their mother with dismay.

Fionn's mother lifted her chin and leveled Elizabeth Beasley with a scathing look. "Cormac was brought to the Tree three months before I was due to give birth to Fionn. He was shown things more terrifying than his worst nightmares. Arranmore cloaked in darkness, a black mountain spearing out of the sea. A shore covered in ash and smoke. He saw the waters of Cowan's Lake run red with islander blood."

She raised her gaze to the ceiling, frowning, as if she was looking for something in the slats. Fionn knew what she was really doing: she was trying not to cry.

"He saw our boy standing against Morrigan before he was even born. He knew—*we* knew—that Fionn was the only one who could face this darkness." Her voice cracked. She pressed her fingers to the base of her throat to keep it from breaking. "Cormac went out in that lifeboat knowing it was part of a greater destiny. The *island's* destiny. He went out knowing he wouldn't come back." She shut her eyes tight. "I knew he wouldn't come back."

Tara folded over herself.

Fionn went still as a statue.

Are you ready, son?

You're the bravest of all of us, you'll see.

"Oh," said his grandfather in a quiet voice. "The lost vision."

The lost vision.

All his life, Fionn had never known the real truth of his father's demise. All the while, his mother had held the secret from him.

She had known his destiny before he took his first breath.

How many more secrets had she kept from him?

She turned to him, her shoulders drooping. "For years I tried to avoid our future. I tried to hide my son from this place. I ran from it. But it followed me to every single apartment we lived in. Every school, every job, every free moment of thought. I was haunted by my husband's last goodbye. By everything he had given up for a better world."

Fionn opened his mouth, closed it again. There was a galaxy churning inside him, constellations of anger and frustration and confusion, and a great black hole in the middle, all the things he thought he knew about his life in Dublin, and his mother, tumbling down inside it.

It was all a lie.

"My husband did not go to his grave so we could hide our heads in the sand and die, one by one," she said to the islanders. "To leave now will damn our island and damn our country. We are *Dagda's* descendants," she said, her fists shaking just as hard as her voice. She was not crying now, but trembling with rage. "The odds might have changed, but we have not. This is our *home*, and we must stand together and fight for its survival."

Fionn had never seen his mother like this. Here was her warrior's heart, still beating after all this time, and in that moment, he hated her for it. For hiding his future from him. For sending him back here, without her.

She sent you to your dad, said a voice inside his head. *She couldn't say goodbye to him twice.*

But she could say goodbye to you, said another voice.

He refused to look at her, turning instead to the crowd, who watched him now with clear eyes—with curiosity. This boy, who had some great unknown future. This boy, who didn't have a lick of magic to show them. He would have to show them his courage instead.

When he addressed the room again, it was with renewed determination. "There is still hope. The descendants know how to use the candles now, and together, we can raise the sea. A wall of water, one hundred times as strong as a ferocious storm. We can sweep the Soulstalkers from the Sea Cave by flooding it, and bring Ivan and the Tide Summoner to us before the sun sets on Arranmore. The shell belongs to the person who found it . . . the person who is truly *worthy* of it. And that's not me," he said, smiling at his friend in the crowd. "It's Shelby Beasley."

Shelby's face lit up with delight, as the other islanders turned to stare at her. "*Really?*" she said breathlessly.

"Are you . . . sure?" said Elizabeth, confusion pinching her brows together. "Shelby is . . ."

"Worthy of it," said Fionn, remembering the way his friend had glowed with the shell in her hands, how the merrow had sung to him of the shell's bond. "I saw it. We both did."

Shelby was beaming so hard, Fionn could see every one of her silver braces. "So I'*ll* blow it then," she said.

"And then the merrows can finish the Soulstalkers off," said Fionn. "Once and for all."

"It just might work," murmured Niall.

"Of course it will," said Fionn's grandfather.

"It has to," said Sam's mother.

"How many candles do we have, Fionn?" asked Donal.

"Enough," was all Fionn said. "For one last stand."

"And what about the islanders who've changed their minds?" asked Douglas.

"I can organize passage from the island for anyone who wishes to leave," said Donal. "We'll have to move quickly and quietly. Children and elderly first. Then the non-descendants."

"That's *cowards'* talk," boomed Tom Rowan. "I don't

need magic to fight. I have my pitchfork. And I'm an islander too!"

"I'm staying right here with my family," said Sam's mother defiantly.

"I'm not a descendant but I'm definitely brave enough to help," said Mia Aguero. "I've been learning judo since I was five!"

"Oh, well, all right," said Juliana reluctantly. "If everyone else is staying, then I'm not going to miss out."

There was a sudden burst of chatter, questions raised and answered in the same breath, panic settling into consideration, and then possibility fell like raindrops, flooding the room with an unmistakeable sense of determination—of *bravery*.

"Take a few minutes to think it over," Fionn said to those who were still chewing on their decision. "I don't want to force this choice on anyone, but our time is running out." He glanced at the wall, where the moon-faced clock ticked over them. "Those who want to leave, go to Donal's house, and he'll arrange passage. For everyone else, we'll start planning in twenty minutes."

Fionn's mother drifted over to him. "Sweetheart . . ."

He pulled his hand away before she could grab it. "I need some air."

The room was moving. Two people stood up. Then

four more. A couple with young children, and a trio of surly teenagers marched out by their mother. A few more from Fionn's class at school. He followed them out of the hall, ducked around the side of the building, and sat in the shadows by the sports shed, staring up at the sky. Evening was hurtling toward them, the sun's rays already reaching for the horizon.

His phone beeped in his pocket—a text from Shelby: **I get to blow the shell!!!!**

Another from Sam: **We are waiting here for you! Ready to fight!! Especially Mom! Ha!**

Shelby again: **I'm so aptly named ☺**

And then Tara: **Where are you? Get back here.**

Sam: **Almost everyone is staying! Even Bartley can't resist those candles!!**

Fionn laid his head back against the wall and listened to the distant chatter of the school hall—islanders and descendants alike, wearing their bravery like battle armor.

I'll go.

Into the storm, whatever that may be.

I'll go.

Just like their ancestors before them.

Just like Cormac Boyle, long lost to the sea.

Fionn squeezed his eyes shut and tried to quell the fluttering in his chest. He didn't know whether he wanted to laugh or cry, only that there was a bird trapped in his rib cage, and it was beating its wings against his heart. His father and his grandfather: a lifeboat and a candle. Bargains made and lives traded for him. All for this strange destiny, this storm that awaited them all.

Another text.

Tara: **Mom feels really bad. Don't make it worse.**

Fionn wasn't trying to make it worse—he was trying to organize his thoughts instead of opening his mouth and erupting like a volcano. He couldn't tell what he was angrier about—that she took him away from here in the first place, or that she sent him back.

He replied to Tara, his fingers flying over the screen: **Coming.**

He stuffed his phone into his pocket and looked up to find a familiar pair of beady eyes peering down at him. "You're still here."

"Where else would I be?" said Elizabeth Beasley. "Isn't this my island too? Shouldn't I want to protect it?"

"I couldn't tell by the way you spoke inside."

Elizabeth smiled sadly. "Come with me, Fionn. I want to show you something."

"What could you possibly have to show me?"

"It's a day for secrets, isn't it?" Elizabeth turned from him, beckoning him across the schoolyard. "I don't want your grandfather to hear us. He'd be very angry at me for interfering."

When Fionn didn't follow her, she glanced over her shoulder.

"It's about his . . . *condition*. I know how to make a new candle that will save him, but the wax is in the attic at my house. It belonged to Bridget Beasley, many years ago. He'd be too proud to ask me for it himself, but he'd listen to you if you gave it to him." Her voice softened. "You're the apple of his eye. You wouldn't even have to tell him where you got it."

Fionn couldn't read her face at this distance. He could only see the swing and shine of her hair as she moved through the school gate. He rolled onto his feet. "Why would you want to help him?" he asked, trailing after her.

"Because I've known your grandfather all my life, Fionn. We have more history between us than you could possibly imagine. No matter what you think of me, my loyalty to this old place runs deeper than my blood. I am an islander first, and a Beasley second."

Fionn's phone beeped in his pocket. "Let's talk about this after the rest of the meeting."

"If you're sure his candle will last," she said, looking over her shoulder. Her eyes shone with the promise of magic, of hope. "Once it goes out, it will be too late to mix the wax."

Sam: **Everyone's waiting for you mate.**

Fionn hovered by the school gate, one foot on either side. "I want to save both of them—Grandad, and the island too."

Elizabeth shrugged. "What if I told you, you *could* do both?"

Fionn glanced back at the school. His phone was ringing in his pocket. He pressed the side button and set it to Silent, before following her down the deserted roadway.

Chapter Twenty-Two

THE BEASLEY BOAT

It was much chillier down by the strand, where the wind brought a skim of frost with it. Elizabeth's strides quickened as the school shrank into the landscape behind them. Fionn jogged after her, his breath making clouds in the air. "Where are we going?"

"You'll see," she said, waving a finger up ahead. "We're almost there."

The thunder of unexpected footsteps announced Bartley's arrival. He caught up with them easily, not a hair out of place. "What's going on?" he demanded. "Where are you going with my gran, Boyle?"

"Bartley, come with us," Elizabeth said, linking her

arm through her grandson's and leading him along the strand. "We're going over to the house for minute."

Bartley screwed his face up in confusion. "You're supposed to be back at that meeting, Boyle. Everyone's waiting for you."

"Hush, Bartley," said Elizabeth sternly. "This is far more important. This is about *family*."

"But—"

"I said hush!" she snapped.

Unease grumbled in Fionn's stomach when they stopped at the lifeboat station. It was bolted shut, and nowhere near Elizabeth's house.

"I'm going back," he said. "Whatever this plan is, it can wait. I'll get my grandfather and we can go together."

Elizabeth ignored him and made a show of patting her coat pockets. "Where is that blasted key? I had it on me this morning."

"Why would you have a key to the lifeboat station?" asked Bartley. "And what are we even doing here?"

Fionn turned to leave.

Elizabeth grabbed him by the sleeve. "Hang on!" she said, her nails digging into his wrist. "You can't go back yet."

"Let go of me," said Fionn, wriggling free.

Elizabeth shuffled backward until she was pressed

against the door of the lifeboat station, like a frightened mouse.

"There's another way to save our family, Bartley," she said, wringing her hands. "Why risk our lives against the Soulstalkers when we can bargain with them?"

Fionn and Bartley exchanged a glance. "What?"

"We're going to stand up and fight, Gran," said Bartley. "That's what we decided."

"Don't be ridiculous. I have our family to think about," she said, her dark eyes blazing. "And in the likely event this goes badly for the island, I'd rather you were safe than dead."

Fionn backed away from her.

Elizabeth stayed where she was. "You know they're not interested in the rest of us, Fionn. They're only interested in you . . ."

"Gran," said Bartley uneasily. "What have you done?"

"This is the price, Bartley. A Beasley boat for a Boyle Storm Keeper. A guaranteed safe passage. *Clemency*."

Fionn slipped his phone from his pocket and scrolled to his sister's number.

"It's too late for heroics now. I've made us a bargain, and we're going to take it."

"A bargain with who?" asked Bartley.

Ivan stepped out from behind the lifeboat station. "Have a guess?"

Fionn pressed the Call button.

Elizabeth lunged for him and knocked the phone out of his hands. It went flying through the air, the screen flashing at him as it disappeared in the long grass.

Fionn turned on his heel and ran.

There was a line of Soulstalkers blocking the road.

"I'm sorry, Fionn. But this is the trade," Elizabeth called after him. "I have to look after my own!"

"Whatever Ivan promised, he lied to you!" said Fionn as the Soulstalkers surrounded him. "You won't be safe, no matter where you go!"

Elizabeth only shook her head, pressing her lips together.

"Bartley! Do something!" shouted Fionn.

But Bartley seemed paralyzed by fear. His jaw hung open, his eyes round with shock.

The Soulstalkers fenced Fionn in as Ivan marched toward him. He grabbed Fionn by the throat, his gloves crackling as Fionn choked the name from his lips. "*Bartl—*"

Bartley just stood there, blinking.

Coward! Fionn screamed inside his head. *Dirty rotten coward!*

His vision was blurring around the edges. He tried to reach for his magic, one final time, but he couldn't feel it, not even the tiniest flicker.

His thoughts became a jumble.

Malachy, Cormac, Fionn.

Fionn, Malachy, Cormac.

The wind was howling.

The earth was trembling.

Cormac, Malachy, Fionn.

"Lights out, Storm Keeper."

Fionn gurgled.

The darkness reached out and buried him in its fist, and his body crumpled to the shuddering earth.

Chapter Twenty-Three

THE CURSED CAULDRON

In the soupy blackness of his mind, Fionn could hear chanting. The words were distorted, garbled by the faraway rush of water. A droplet landed on his cheek and slithered into his hair.

Tick-tock, watch the clock.

Tick-tock, crumbling rock.

His thoughts flitted by like moths, the wings crushed to dust before he could catch hold of them.

Where am I?

Fionn twitched. He was lying on something cold and soft. Sand, slicked with mist. There was water nearby; waves that spat the scent of seaweed into the air and blew froth up his nose. Slowly he became aware of his body—his arms half crushed beneath him, his legs bent away from each other.

"Wakey-wakey, Storm Keeper!" came Ivan's voice. He kicked him sharply in the ribs. "Get up!"

Fionn raised his face from the sand, and found himself in the middle of a cove. The sun had long surrendered to the horizon, and in its place the moon was rising. It was the only beacon of light in a starless sky. Up above, the craggy cliffs peered over him, straining for their reflections in the waves. Fionn groaned as he turned, his neck creaking with the effort. Everywhere he looked, hungry eyes peered back at him. A colosseum of Soulstalkers come to watch him bleed.

"Look alive, Keeper." Ivan dragged Fionn to his feet by the scruff of his neck, and pulled him along behind him. "The solstice is upon us."

Fionn's eyes adjusted quickly, first to the darkening night . . . and then to the three onyx shards glistening in the distance. *Black Point Rock*. They were in Hughie Rua's Cove. On one end of the crescent-shaped bay, a mound of sea-slimed rocks climbed up toward the cliffs, and on the other end, much too close for comfort, the Sea Cave lay buried inside the rock.

The Soulstalkers streamed around him, filling every inch of Hughie's little cove. Some carried big hulking rocks with them, stacking them on top of each other to make a rudimentary parapet, while two burly men dragged a cauldron across the sand. It was wide and thick, and hewn from stone—over half Fionn's size and certainly twice as heavy. They heaved it up onto their makeshift altar, settling it with a thud that sent something dark sloshing over the rim. Fionn tasted the sudden tang of copper in the air.

They paused at the base of the parapet. "The tide is still out," said Ivan, turning to leer at him. "Even the sea is afraid of us."

It was then that Fionn noticed the Tide Summoner hanging from his neck.

Ivan crooked his finger and Fionn was shoved up onto the rocks. The Soulstalker climbed up after him, curling his fingers around the back of his neck. "Beautiful solstice," he crooned. "A night to die. A night to *live*."

Before Fionn could form a proper thought, let alone a *plan*, he was bent roughly over the cauldron's rim. Smoke shot up his nose and into his mouth, and he retched. The liquid rippled, plumes of gray turning cloudy white, as a man's face appeared in the center. It was long and thin and made of angles. He looked, disconcertingly, like Ivan, only he was much older. Under a slim red beard, he had that same sloping mouth. His keen eyes were swollen with pupils. They blinked at Fionn, growing bigger as he loomed closer.

The tang of copper grew stronger. Fionn's head was spinning so fast, he couldn't see straight. The cauldron had its own strange brand of magic. Just like Cowan's Lake, it had recorded its memories, only these were full of dark magic. It was making him sick.

The man turned sharply to something over his shoulder, and then everything turned red, the icy planes of his face disappearing in rivers of blood. The cauldron hiccuped and a young woman appeared. She was pale and wan, with wide gray eyes. Fionn knew them too well—darkened and empty, they had bored into him once before on an ancient beach.

Fionn was so entranced by the strangeness of Morrigan trapped inside the cauldron that he forgot the Soulstalker looming over him. Ivan reached over his shoulder and dangled the Tide Summoner by its rim. "Let's start with this, shall we? Seeing as you won't be needing it."

"NO!" Fionn choked on his scream as the shell tumbled into the cauldron. The liquid hissed, soupy rivers of black rising up to claim it. And all the while Ivan held him still, his fingers like a vise around his neck.

The Tide Summoner disappeared slowly into the

cauldron until there was nothing but blood-black oil bubbling below him. Ivan withdrew a knife from his pocket. It glinted in the corner of Fionn's eye as he brought it to the back of his neck. Fionn squirmed against the lip of the cauldron. He tried to reach into the hole in his chest, to hook a tendril of that weeping magic and call it up from the depths of him.

Please, he implored.

Don't let this be the end.

Please.

Ivan brought his lips to his ear. "Try not to squirm too much."

There was nothing now but the taste of smoke on the back of his tongue, the glug-glugging of the cauldron as it began to lick Dagda's magic from the Tide Summoner.

Dagda help me.

I beg you.

Fionn felt the blade press against his neck, a half second before the world exploded.

Ivan screamed as the ground was ripped out from under them. They were flung backward into a spray of shale and sand and falling rock. Fionn freewheeled through the air, thrown out toward the sea, where he landed in the shallows with a heavy *splat!* He pressed his cheek to the sand, narrowly avoiding the cauldron as it whooshed over his head and landed with an almighty *crash!*

Amidst the chaos, a familiar voice rang out. “Happy solstice, you bloody monsters! Who’s got my grandson?”

Fionn raised his head from the froth and blinked into the shifting moonlight. The dust was clearing. His grandfather marched right through it.

“Let me impart this precious kernel of wisdom in what will surely be your final moments in this world.” He raised his hand to the quivering earth. “Hell hath *no* fury like a grandad scorned.”

The second blast ripped the cliffs apart.

Chapter Twenty-Four

THE SINKING SOULSTALKER

The beach exploded, bones cracking and bodies thudding as the cliffs rushed to meet them. Overhead, the moon swelled in the night sky, as though it was coming down to take a closer look. Blood-curdling screams filled the little cove as Soulstalkers scrabbled to unbury themselves from the crumbling earth. Fionn's grandfather blasted a pathway right through it.

He stopped on the edge of the ocean with raw fury in his eyes. "Come out of the sea, lad!" He waved his candle, the flame crawling up inside it as he marched along the sand. "Show your sniveling face, Ivan. We want our Tide Summoner back!"

Fionn limped through the shallows, staring at his grandfather in dawning alarm.

Malachy Boyle had ripped the anchor from his own candle and turned it upside down.

He was burning up the very essence of his life and turning it to pure, undiluted power.

"Grandad, no!"

Fionn's grandfather wasn't listening. He was too busy scouring the beach, upturning groaning Soulstalkers and flinging them into the sky like leaves.

"Where are you, Ivan?" Fionn's grandfather yelled. "Come out and fight me, you creepy little insect!"

Fionn's magic flickered in his chest—it was an ember buried in a cavern of icy fear, but it was enough to get his attention. To turn his head. The Tide Summoner was nearby. He could *feel* it. He scanned the shoreline, his chest growing warmer as he stumbled through the shallows, until... *There!* Just up ahead! The shell glinted bone-white in the moonlight, a stone's throw from where the cauldron was wedged into the damp sand.

Fionn ignored the stiffness in his limbs and sprinted toward it, just as a Soulstalker emerged from a pile of rubble and launched herself in his direction.

Fionn leaped through the air, falling on the shell like

it was a bomb about to explode. "I've got it!" he yelled. "It's here, Grandad!"

"Take it with you!" his grandfather shouted. "Get back to safety!"

Fionn tried to run, but the Soulstalker grabbed him by the back of his sweater and elbowed him in the ribs, yanking the Tide Summoner from his grasp.

Fionn pulled her by the hair, tussling back and forth for it. "Give it to me!"

"Watch out, lad!"

Suddenly the ground cracked in two. The sand burrowed into itself, forging a gaping chasm between them. Fionn scrambled away, just as the Soulstalker slipped into the hole. She reached out in a panic, grappling at nothing.

Fionn plunged his hand into the sinkhole and felt the shift of gravity pulling him down. He ripped the Tide Summoner from her hand, throwing himself backward before the hole could claim him too. The Soulstalker screamed as she disappeared—the last streaks of her brassy hair lost to the shifting sands. It covered her in a golden wave, the ground belching as it gulped her down.

And then she was gone.

"FIONN!"

Tara and Sam skidded to a stop on the edge of the crumbling cliff.

"FOUND THEM," screamed Tara, over her shoulder, while Sam waved a candle back and forth.

"Climb up to us, mate! Hurry! We'll hold them back with the wind!"

Relief rushed through Fionn. He slung the Tide Summoner around his neck and took the first steps toward freedom.

Behind him, across the cove, his grandfather stumbled.

Chapter Twenty-Five

THE STORM KEEPER'S SACRIFICE

Fionn hovered on the slip of sand between the Atlantic Ocean and his battered island, and felt the Tide Summoner's pulse thumping against his own.

His heart was splitting in two.

His grandfather had dropped to his knees. The moon poured its silvery light over him as the Soulstalkers crawled out from the rubble and fanned around him like the wings of an avenging angel. Ivan was at their helm, grinning from ear to ear. The candle in Fionn's grandfather's fist was gone, its magic spattered in gray puddles along his hand.

"Get up the steps, mate!" shouted Sam. "Shelby's almost here!"

"They've got Grandad!" Fionn yelled back. "They're going to kill him!"

"You have to come back up, Fionn!" shouted Tara. "He knew, Fionn! He knew what he was doing!"

Fionn unwound the Tide Summoner from his neck and drew his arm back as he ran toward them. He threw the shell with all his might, his breath hitching as he watched it sail through the darkness, landing halfway down the rocky slope. Sam lowered himself onto the slick rubble, his knees shaking as he took the rocks two at a time.

"Watch my back!" yelled Fionn as he turned and sprinted in the opposite direction, his heartbeat thundering in his ears.

"FIONN! NO!" screamed Tara.

Fionn only moved faster, picking his way through the mounting rubble. Across the cove, the Sea Cave yawned at the sky, its shell cracked like a broken egg. The Soulstalkers were crawling out from the toppled cliffs and crowding around its crumbled walls. They didn't turn their heads to look for Fionn, only pressed themselves tight to the rock as it made echoes of Ivan's commands.

"Come on, old man. *Move*," he hissed.

Fionn recognized the cursed cauldron as it was hoisted onto a tower of rubble. It was battered and cracked and coated in wet sand, but there was smoke still churning above it. Whatever curse it wore hadn't been broken. Fionn watched in horror as his grandfather was pushed up after it, then shoved roughly to his knees.

"Get down!" hissed Ivan. "Hurry up!"

His knife glinted menacingly in the moonlight.

"Stop!" Fionn shouted as he ran. "Let him go!"

His grandfather tried to raise his head. "F-Fionn? Is that you?"

Ivan looked up. The explosion had ripped his right ear off, and singed a jagged line through his beard. "See how our magic helps him?" He raised his grandfather's head so Fionn could see the recognition in his glassy eyes. "See how he knows you without his tricks?"

"Fionn," his grandfather rasped. "Get out of here. Get back up the cliff!"

"Retreat as you like," grinned Ivan. "I only need one of you."

He slammed Fionn's grandfather's head back into the cauldron, his fingers twined in the collar of his blue sweater. "Storm Keepers," he said, peering over the cauldron now. "As it turns out, this one was easier to catch. Honestly, I don't know *how* I missed it before. He *reeks* of magic."

She will rise when the Storm Keeper bleeds for her.

All of a sudden, Rose's words swam through Fionn's mind.

You are a Keeper once, you are a Keeper forever.

Ivan brought the knife down and slashed a deep line along his grandfather's cheek. He slumped into the cauldron's mouth.

NO!

A firestorm erupted in every corner of Fionn's body, a blazing heat beginning in his toes, twisting and swelling up through his legs and into his arms, until it felt as if he might burst into a million pieces.

The ground exploded around him. Soulstalkers were thrown into the air like confetti, the knife flung from Ivan's grip. He was thrown backward, releasing Fionn's grandfather and tumbling down the rocks with the cauldron crashing after him.

Fionn didn't break his advance. His vision clouded with red mist as debris cycloned around him, picking up shells and seaweed and pebbles and rocks. He shot them at Ivan like bullets, snapped spires of rock from the broken cliffs, and spun them through the air.

There was a voice whispering inside Fionn's head, a needle stitching his magic to his rage until he couldn't tell where one ended and the other began. He could sense the link now; his unchecked emotion was the true source of his power. His loyalty. His love.

This, his magic seemed to say. *This is how it works.*

Not with your head, but with your heart.

"You had no magic!" screamed Ivan, his hands coming to his face as the cauldron rolled over him, the thick, dark liquid spilling out onto the rocky sand. "You're broken!"

Fionn was not broken. And he wasn't finished either.

The lightning came with a fresh torrent of rage. It ripped through Fionn's heart, filling his body with fizzing white heat. He screamed as it sparked from his mouth and his eyes and his ears and his fingers, spearing through the world in a jagged bolt. Not wielded, but *created*. Borne of his soul.

It smashed through the cauldron, shattering it to smithereens before slamming into the Soulstalker's chest.

Ivan was skewered in a single, deafening blast, every inch of him burned up in a thick curl of smoke.

Incinerated.

Just as the ground began to tremble.

Chapter Twenty-Six

THE RAVEN QUEEN

The cauldron liquid bubbled as it devoured the earth. Dark magic seeped from the ground like a noxious gas, turning the air around Fionn thick and wavy. His grandfather was on his knees, trying to crawl through it. "Cormac?" he rasped. "Are you there, Cormac?"

Fionn pressed his sleeve over his mouth and leaped over the creaking rock. "I'm right here!"

He dragged his grandfather to his feet, shouldering his weight as he led him back toward the beach. "This way. Hurry!"

The darkness curled at their backs.

"Don't turn around," said Fionn. "Just keep moving."

The surviving Soulstalkers peeled backward, streaming into the shallow water. There they stood, shoulder to shoulder, bringing hands to damaged faces. Their tattoos were glowing silver, as though moonlight was bleeding from their skin.

"She's rising!"

"At last, the Raven Queen returns!"

"What's going on?" muttered Fionn's grandfather. "Who are these people, Cormac?"

"Just keep moving." Fionn gritted his teeth. "We need to get away from here."

"Fionn! Hurry!" came Tara's voice from overhead. "If we raise the tide now, we'll drown you!"

"Don't look back!" yelled Sam, as he sent a gust of wind to hurry them along. "Just keep going!"

The rest of the islanders had gathered up on the cliffside now, candles readied in their grasp. Shelby was picking her way down the rocks, waving the Tide Summoner back and forth. "You can do it, Fionn!"

Fionn felt the gathering dark like a hand on his shoulder, pressing him into the earth. His grandfather was a second weight. His feet were barely dragging on the sand now. "Let me go, Cormac," he murmured. "Let me lie down."

"Not yet," grunted Fionn. "Not at her feet."

The sand thumped and then rippled like a carpet. Fionn was knocked to his knees, his grandfather coming down heavily on him.

Across the cove, a gaping hole appeared in the earth.

Out of it came a flock of shrieking ravens.

And out of the ravens walked Morrigan.

Fionn's grandfather gripped his wrist. "Dagda save us all," he breathed.

Morrigan.

The word traveled along the headland, leaping in and out of fearful mouths.

Down in the cove, it carried a different meaning.

Queen.

Leader.

Keeper of our souls.

It was awe.

Redemption.

Joy.

The Soulstalkers fell to their knees and pressed their faces to the damp sand. They glowed like beacons of light, their strength beginning to return to them. Their purpose reignited after all this time.

The Raven Queen has risen.

All hail the Raven Queen.

The birds splintered into the sky, leaving Morrigan

alone on the beach. She unfolded her limbs in a series of loud clicks, straightening her spine and cracking her fingers, one by one. Then she rolled her neck around and settled her gaze on Fionn.

Fionn felt it like a bullet in his chest. He spun, scanning the rocks. Shelby was holding the Tide Summoner against her chest, her horror a perfect mirror of his own.

"Blow it!" he shouted.

"I can't, Fionn—you'll drown!"

"*Now!*" he roared.

He turned to his grandfather. "Run for those rocks, Grandad," he said urgently. "Crawl if you have to, and climb quickly—the people up there will help you." His mother was already slipping her way down to help. "I'm going to keep Morrigan down here, on the beach."

Fionn's grandfather gripped him harder. "What are you talking about, Cor—"

"*Go!*" said Fionn, pushing him away.

He turned from him, and before fear could change his mind or send him running just the same, Fionn marched toward Morrigan.

Her cape of souls trailed along the sand behind her. The solstice moon threaded shards of silvery light through it, while the strain of her movements flickered in her jaw. She was stiff, weak.

She stopped before him. "It has been a long time, Storm Keeper."

Fionn eyed the folds of her cloak. The souls shifted—their mouths twisted in agony, eyes wide with eternal pain. "I can't say I'm glad for the reunion."

Morrigan blinked too slowly, blood-red capillaries wiring the paper-thin skin around her eyes. "And yet you've come to greet me."

Fionn reached for his magic, but found only fear guttering inside him. Dread was tight as a noose around his neck as his grandfather scrabbled up the cliffs behind him. "I thought it might be nice to kill you," said Fionn, stalling for time. "The same way I killed your brother, Ivan, just now."

Morrigan's smile dissolved. She shot her hand out and seized him by the throat, choking the breath from him in an audible *whoosh!*

Fionn's body lit up like a fuse. Every inch of him was on fire, his magic scalding him from the inside out. It railed against Morrigan's shadows as her fingers closed around his windpipe.

Someone screamed his name.

Morrigan brought her nose close to his, her dark eyes glittering with curiosity. "Dagda?" she whispered.

Fionn closed his hands around her wrists. "Let go," he gurgled.

Morrigan tugged him closer, sniffing the air around his face.

"What is this?" she hissed. "What *are* you?"

Fionn dug his fingernails into her icy skin as a gust of wind tried to cleave them apart.

"I can't get her!" yelled Tara.

Another gust smashed into them—this one stronger than the last. The islanders were banding together, but it wasn't enough to shake Fionn free. Morrigan only tightened her grip. "You are not what I thought you were, little Keeper. Not then, and not now."

Fionn was lifted up into the air. His feet dangled below him, his hands like cuffs around her wrists.

"I'll use you before I kill you. What you took from me, you will return twofold." She turned and marched into the waves, swinging him like a puppet from a string.

Far away, the Tide Summoner rang out, clear as an ancient, haunting knell.

It followed them into the ocean, where it skimmed the water like a stone before disappearing into its depths.

Chapter Twenty-Seven

THE NINTH WAVE

The sea was swelling. Morrigan pushed through it, dragging Fionn behind her. He thrashed and twisted in her grasp, his heels scraping along the seabed as he glimpsed the cove behind them. There were so many faces staring after them, horrified islanders stuck on the cliffs, tattooed bodies glowing along the shore, and there, lumbering across the sand all by himself . . . Fionn's grandfather.

"ONE!" cried a voice from the cliffs.

Shelby.

Fionn tried to grab hold of the name as Morrigan's cape shuttered around him.

He tumbled over himself, swallowing a fistful of saltwater.

"Dagda," Morrigan hissed, her eyes on the rising tide. "Here, even when he's not."

"TWO!" came a faraway voice.

Shelby, Fionn reminded himself.

Shelby was calling the tide home.

Eight waves to call the tide,

On the ninth wave, the merrows ride.

Nine waves. Nine waves and they would have an army.

Morrigan halted, as another wave crashed into them. It brought the water to Fionn's hips. Already the horizon was brewing another one.

"THREE!" yelled the distant voice.

"My Stags," she hissed again. Fionn didn't have to turn around to see; he could feel their nearness in the hairs on his neck. "*My brothers.*"

Another wave crashed into them.

"FOUR!"

The tide climbed to Fionn's chest.

Morrigan's cape lifted into the air, the patchwork of contorted faces taking flight around Fionn. They stroked the notches in his spine and whispered their screams into his ears.

"Let us see what Dagda's shadow can do." She began to mutter—a string of deep, guttural sounds that choked out of her. Her jaw dislocated with a sickening *click!* and shadows streamed from her gullet in thick, dark plumes. They plunged into Fionn's open mouth. He heaved violently, his body screaming as they rushed down his throat. The icy tentacles wound through his bloodstream, prodding, twisting, *searching*. They found the flame inside him, and took it. They licked the heat from between the bones of his rib cage, swallowing his magic in desperate, greedy gulps.

"FIVE!"

Fionn was lost in bone-shuddering agony. He had become a black hole, his mouth and his chest and his mind blown wide open to the darkness.

Take it. Take it all. Just let it be over.

There was an almighty *crack!* from somewhere over his shoulder. Morrigan roared as the first rock split in two. "BREDON!"

Her cape billowed, the folds shifting to reveal the image of a brute male with a crimson eye. The ruby glinted at Fionn, as he pulled his lips back and bared his teeth like a wolf. He had Ivan's sharp cheekbones and the same dark gaze, but his neck was thicker, the veins in his forehead moving like worms under his skin.

"SIX!" came a voice from the strand. Fionn was sure he recognized it, but he couldn't catch the name as it flitted by. He couldn't remember what the number meant.

There was sea salt on his tongue and water around his neck now. The shadows were still rifling through his insides, licking away the light. Soon there would be nothing left.

He could feel the emptiness yawning inside him.

The second *crack!* made the sea tremble.

The face was already waiting in the shadows, watching Fionn. It had the same violent eyes and pallid skin, but there was no smile, no teeth bared like a rabid animal. His mouth had been sewn shut, his bloodless lips bound together with thick black twine.

"ALDRIC!"

Aldric the Silent. Aldric, with his mouth sewn up.

Fionn began to shudder. There was so little of him left now—the barest flicker of light hiding in the recesses of his bones. Soon, there would be nothing but a dry, soulless husk.

"SEVEN!"

A wave slammed into him, and he was knocked free of Morrigan's grasp. The darkness faltered and his thoughts rushed back in.

"KEEP FIGHTING IT, LAD!" Through a crack in the dark, Fionn heard his grandfather's voice. "DON'T GIVE UP!"

He remembered then—his own name.

Fionn.

His purpose.

Survive.

"My Queen!" came a chorus of shrieks. "The tide!"

Fionn launched for the shore but Morrigan was on him in a heartbeat. Her cape surrounded him again, her shadows coming thick and fast, but this time Fionn held on to himself. He shut his eyes and concentrated on his grandfather's words, the sound of his own name. He found that kernel of light deep in his chest and curled his mind around it.

"Keep fighting it, lad!"

His magic flared.

Morrigan hissed.

The warmth in his chest spread to his shoulders, and then his arms. Morrigan's shadows grew clumsier, prodding with urgency—desperation. She was muttering under her breath. Fionn held on to his grandfather's voice, to the memory of him blasting the beach apart to save him. He squeezed tighter and tighter, until his magic crawled up his throat, and Morrigan snapped her hand away with a blood-curdling shriek.

"EIGHT!" yelled Shelby, and Fionn remembered her too.

The eighth wave swept over them with the force of a

high-speed train, and he surrendered to it. They were blown apart from each other, into a sea of churning froth. Fionn let himself sink down, down, down, away from the shadows, away from the darkness, and into the quiet, endless water.

In the depths, the current sang him a lullaby.

Eight waves to call the tide,

On the ninth wave, the merrows ride.

An arm came around his middle.

Fionn was pulled up through the waves, breaking the surface in a sucking gasp.

"Swim!" shouted his grandfather. "Swim with me, Cormac!"

"NINE!" yelled a distant voice. "*The ninth wave!*"

Fionn swam, and the final wave came after them, like a stampede. The tide was so high it careened over the Soulstalkers and climbed up the cliffs. They were pedaling just as desperately as Fionn, half of them yelling for their Queen, the others swimming for the cave tunnels.

"The merrows are coming!" yelled Shelby.

The wave hurled Fionn and his grandfather toward the cliffside. Under Tara's command, the islanders reached down and curled a fist of wind around them. They were pulled up from the roiling sea, their arms and legs splayed out like starfish.

They were blown over the cliff edge, where they floated like balloons, until Fionn's mother and Sam's father pulled them down by their legs. They rolled onto the grass in two identical heaps, crumpled but alive. Both gasping for air. The islanders blew out their candles and scattered their gust of wind, just in time to watch the sea explode.

The ocean spat out its warriors in a deafening cry. The merrows leaped from the waves like dolphins, their shining eyes bright as the full moon. With Lír leading her army, they moved through the water like scythes, their sharp-toothed mouths gnashing at the ravens that tried to beat them back.

Fionn crawled to the edge of the broken cliffs and watched in terrified wonder as the merrows made quick work of their prey, descending on the flailing Soulstalkers and dragging them down into the depths of the ocean. Their teeth cut through bones as if through butter, their lithe arms snapped limbs and necks and rib cages. Those who broke away were herded back, spun inside an endless whirlpool until they drowned in the froth.

For a long time, the sky sang with the screams of dying Soulstalkers. The islanders watched from the cliff-side as the merrows rose up from the annals of history and brought their reign of terror to the ocean's surface. They dived and shrieked and swam and fought until the sea fell eerily still. Until there were no faces bobbing on the surface, no hands reaching up through the waves.

"Terrifying," murmured Fionn's mother.

The merrows circled the empty ocean, their tails shining like jewels in the moonlight.

"I did that," said Shelby from where her legs dangled over the cliffside. "I called them, and they came. For *me*."

Fionn knew what she was really saying.

I *belong*.

She was right.

But what about him? What of this strange magic inside him? This thing that so rarely answered to him, that took even Morrigan by surprise? Far ahead, the jagged edges of Black Point Rock rose into the sky. The fissures were near invisible from here, the seas around them deceptively calm, but Fionn had heard the stone rupture, and knew those tombs were no longer sealed.

"Fionn?" Tara tapped Fionn on the shoulder. "Can you get up? It's Grandad. There's something wrong with him."

Fionn rolled onto his feet.

"He won't talk to any of us," said Tara, leading him across the grass. "I don't think he knows who we are."

Fionn's heart sank at the sight of his grandfather. He was sitting alone on the headland, cast in the moon's spot-light. He had tucked his knees up to his chest and was holding his head in his hands. The last of his magic had finally deserted him.

He had survived, only to die.

"Say something to him," whispered Tara.

Fionn dropped to a squat and placed a hand on his grandfather's arm. He could hear the faint whistle as he took in breath. "Grandad? It's me, Fionn."

His grandfather raised his head. There was a deep red gash along his cheek, and behind his cracked spectacles, his eyes were full of clouds. "I don't know any Fionn."

Fionn's mother joined them; her face was drawn, the crinkles around her mouth much deeper than before. "What about Cormac?" she said softly. "Do you remember Cormac, Malachy?"

Fionn's grandfather settled his head into the cradle of his arms and stared at the grass between his knees. "I don't know Cormac," he said in a muffled voice. "I don't know anyone."

A fissure zigzagged through Fionn's heart—a new lightning bolt in an old storm.

Tara crouched down beside him. "He's dying, isn't he?" she said, close to his ear.

Fionn didn't want to answer her.

"Yes," he said eventually. "I think so."

"So . . . this is the end then?" she whispered.

"Yes," said Fionn.

"Are you *sure*?"

Fionn turned on her. "*Yes*," he said angrily. "Open your eyes!"

"Fionn," chastised their mother.

Tara sniffed, and reached into her pocket. "Then I'm supposed to give you something," she said. "It's from Rose. She was here earlier."

She opened her fist to reveal a candle. It was a perfect spiral, rendered in winding swirls of green and violet.

Fionn stared at the wax as it rolled along his sister's palm.

"Do you know what it is, Fionn?" asked his mother.

He took the candle from Tara. It was warm against his skin, the wax gleaming with one last sprinkle of impossibility.

Aurora Borealis.

"Yes," he said quietly. "I know what it is."

Chapter Twenty-Eight

AURORA BOREALIS

"Can I borrow your lighter?" asked Fionn.

His mother patted her coat pockets. "I thought I had two," she said, frowning. "I must have given my last one to Niall."

"Sam took mine," said Tara, looking around her. "He's over there with his parents."

Fionn's mother turned on her heel. "I'll find one," she said, marching away.

Fionn stared at the candle with prickling eyes. Then at his grandfather, still frozen on the grass.

A hand appeared above him, a silver lighter dangling from two fingers. "You can use mine."

It was Bartley. He looked worse than Fionn had ever

seen him—his hair stuck up in every direction, as if he had been electrocuted. His eyes were red-rimmed, and his skin was paler than the moon watching over them.

Fionn made no move to take the lighter. The last time he was this close to Bartley Beasley, he was getting choked and carted off by Soulstalkers. Now Morrigan had risen and his grandfather was dying.

"Shouldn't you be on the mainland with your gran by now?"

"My family decided to stay," said Bartley stiffly. "My gran's back at home."

"Licking her wounds then."

"Just take it," said Bartley, dropping the lighter on the grass.

"Tell her she got what she wanted," said Fionn bitterly. "Her precious boat in exchange for the ruin of Arranmore. You might as well use it."

Bartley glared at him. "I didn't know what she was up to, Boyle. I think that was pretty obvious."

"You *let* them take me."

"What else was I supposed to do?" snapped Bartley. "Kick up a fuss and get dragged off with you?"

"Coward," spat Fionn.

"*Fionn*," said Tara. "Bartley's the one who told us what happened. He followed Ivan here and then came back to tell Grandad. We wouldn't have found you so fast if it wasn't for him."

"Why is it that he's always involved in our kidnappings?" said Fionn pointedly. "Constantly tattling, but never rescuing."

"He tried to make it right," said Tara. "He's here, isn't he?"

Fionn turned on her. "Morrigan has *risen*. Or did you *miss* that part?"

"What a luxury it must be to have a family who believes in all the same things that you do," said Bartley, turning on his heel and stalking back across the grass to where Shelby was still sitting on the edge of the cliff, enamored of her sea-ful of merrows.

Tara picked up the lighter. "There are worse people out there than Bartley, you know."

"You can have more than one enemy," said Fionn.

"Not right now you can't." She looked meaningfully at their grandfather. "You're just choosing to be angry so you won't have to be sad."

She was right. It was easier to be angry at Bartley than heartbroken over his grandfather.

"Whatever," he mumbled.

"Are you ready?" she said, handing him the lighter. "We can go together."

Fionn passed the candle to Tara and wound his

fingers in his grandfather's hand. He let him do it, his grip limp as a dead fish. On the other side, Tara did the same.

With a heavy heart, Fionn flicked the lighter open.

Tara brought the wick to the flame, and *Aurora Borealis* lit up with a faint *whoosh!*

They held on tight to their grandfather as the wind spun them into another layer. The islanders dissolved and Fionn imagined what they must look like—a grandfather and his grandchildren, melting away just the same. They huddled around the flame as the wind busied itself pulling layers through the skies and stitching new ones underneath their feet.

The grass grew tall around their ankles. The sea shrank, and swallowed the merrows, and the Sea Cave groaned as it put itself back together, rock by rock. The moon was smudged from the sky, the starless obsidian brushed to navy.

Clouds churned around the edges, and the first luminous brushstroke shimmered into being—it was green as the island grass, green as a precious emerald. An owl *hoo-hoo*'d from a nearby tree, welcoming them to a very different Arranmore, where they sat alone on a deserted headland underneath a glowing sky.

As though waking from a deep sleep, Fionn's grandfather raised his head and blinked at Fionn. There was a moment of nothingness, and then his smile grew, the edges curling as his eyes turned a brilliant, blazing blue. "Hello, stranger."

"Hello, Grandad."

He turned to Tara, who was doing her very best not to cry. "You look a little glum, love."

"Just a bit," she sniffed.

He turned back to Fionn, his gaze lingering on the ring of bruises around his throat. "And you look a little the worse for wear, lad."

Fionn smiled weakly. "I've seen better days."

"I suppose I have too." His grandfather crossed his eyes at the crack in his spectacles. "Though I confess I can't fully remember this one."

"That's probably for the best," said Tara.

Fionn could feel grief coming for him. Somewhere in the back of his mind, another clock was ticking.

"Will you walk with us, Grandad?" he said, rising to his feet.

His grandfather looked at his hands entwined in theirs, noted the candle blazing in Tara's fist. A shadow passed behind his eyes, gone as quickly as it came.

"Yes," he said. "I'll walk with you."

They helped him stand up, his knees creaking in the silence. The breeze was soft against their backs, gently guiding them as they ambled onward, three wanderers bathed in green light. Fionn had never witnessed a night so iridescent with magic. He had never felt quite so connected with the ancient power of this place, and yet it left an aching sadness in the deepest part of him.

His grandfather seemed to be having the very same thought. “Phosphorescent skies,” he said wistfully. “For ten years, I’ve dreamed of this night.”

Fionn heard the words he didn’t say.

I know this night.

I know this end.

He didn’t feel like replying. Neither, it seemed, did Tara.

The moment was so perfect, Fionn was afraid he might shatter it with the truth of what they had left behind—what they would have to return to, without their grandfather to guide them. They walked a while in silence, the breeze frittering about their ankles. The owl followed overhead, its dappled wings gleaming turquoise underneath the Northern Lights.

“What aching beauty,” said Fionn’s grandfather in a faraway voice. “I think if I could do it all again, I would spend more time outside.”

“You spent most of your life outdoors,” said Tara.

“Passing through it,” he said, his head still tipped back. “The magic was all around me and I never really stopped to take it in.”

Before long, they found themselves in the heartland of Arranmore. The grass grew wilder, the meadows laden with thick-headed purple flowers that swayed back and forth; saying hello, saying goodbye.

The sky was purple too. It chased the green around the stars, soaked the Milky Way in glowing violet. The wind changed and Fionn felt those invisible hands against his chest.

"Fionn?" said Tara, at that same moment.

They slowed to a stop.

Their grandfather pulled his gaze from the sky. "What is it?"

Fionn noticed the crack in his spectacles had been repaired. There was color in his cheeks again, the skin soft and new where his cut had been. The lines had been smoothed from his forehead, and Fionn could see a light dusting of dark hair on the top of his head.

He glanced at the candle. The wax was streaming over Tara's fingers. "I don't think we can go any farther," he said. "I think this is where we're supposed to leave you."

His grandfather frowned. "Oh."

Tara nodded at the ground. "Sorry, Grandad."

Fionn's grief was in his throat now, making his tongue heavy in his mouth.

"Well, of course you two can't come with me," said his

grandfather, rolling his shoulders back and shedding the skin of his melancholy. He cleared his throat gruffly. "That would be very silly indeed. You both have entire *lives* to lead."

Do we? thought Fionn.

"You haven't eaten a whole ice-cream cake for dinner or had a two-day-old pizza for breakfast yet," said his grandfather. "Nor have you bought a single turtle *or* bunny rabbit for no good reason."

"No," said Tara sadly.

"You haven't failed your driving test at least once."

"We're too young to drive," said Fionn.

"You haven't driven a tractor all the way to Dublin, only to end up in Galway by accident."

"I wouldn't do that," said Tara. "I'd use Google Maps."

"You haven't fallen in love yet," said his grandfather, winking at Fionn.

Fionn felt his cheeks burn. "E*w*."

Tara giggled. "I have."

Fionn grimaced. "I might vomit."

"You haven't written a terrible love poem for someone and then suffocated in your own embarrassment when their father finds it instead and reads it out at Sunday mass," their grandfather went on serenely. "You haven't experienced the hellish poison that is airplane coffee."

"*Should* we?" asked Tara.

"Of *course* you should," he said, with such certainty Fionn added it immediately to the top of his bucket list. "You haven't wandered into a St. Patrick's Day parade and ended up accidentally leading the procession."

"How did you even . . . ?" Fionn trailed off.

"You haven't known the immense joy of having a child who is *exactly* as perfect and handsome as you. And then grandchildren—*oh*, they are the real treasure," he said, smiling broadly. "For goodness sake, neither of you have ever been arrested."

"Well, um, no," said Fionn.

His grandfather peered at each of them over the bridge of his spectacles. "And do either of you know what income tax is?"

They shook their heads.

"Try to avoid that last one for as long as you can," he said gravely. "It withers the soul."

"Okay," said Fionn.

"We will," said Tara.

The wind was picking up. The flame grew higher in warning.

Fionn cleared his throat; he tried to pretend he wasn't crying, but his cheeks were wet and his eyes were stinging.

His grandfather's cheeks were wet too. "Oh dear," he said quietly. "My eyes are leaking."

"Same," whispered Tara.

Fionn hiccuped. "Mine too."

"Must be the flowers."

"Yeah."

"Definitely."

Their grandfather's smile began to wobble. "Am I still handsome, though?"

"Yes, of course," said Tara quickly.

"You're always handsome," said Fionn.

In fact, Fionn had never seen his grandfather look so handsome.

"Are you two too old to hug your grandfather?" he said, squeezing their hands. "Or can I have one for the road?"

Fionn and Tara curled into their grandfather so fast they bumped heads. Tara flung her free arm around Fionn, the candle burning just above his shoulder, until they were all huddled together. Their grandfather laid his head on top of theirs. His sweater was scratchy against Fionn's face, the thick blue threads mottled with sea salt and adventure.

The air grew warmer, the breeze wrapping its arms around them as grief seeped out of their hearts and made them weep. There were droplets on the wind, the distant cry of faraway gulls carried with it, and Fionn thought perhaps the island was weeping too.

Their grandfather lifted his head first, his eyes

shining behind his spectacles. He turned to Tara and pressed a kiss into the crown of her head.

"Goodbye, love," he murmured. "You're a wonder."

Tara passed the candle to Fionn. He took it with his free hand, lurching as the wind cut through him. The memory held firm around them, like a bubble.

"Goodbye, Grandad," sobbed Tara.

"Be brave," he said, kissing her hand, and then releasing it. "And look after each other."

"Always."

The wind carried her away.

Fionn's grandfather turned to him then.

Fionn's bottom lip was quivering so badly, he couldn't speak.

His grandfather laid a heavy hand on his shoulder, his sadness dissolving for a fleeting moment. "Listen to me carefully, lad."

Fionn went very still as the candle flame thrashed in his fist.

"Now that Morrigan has risen, she will be much harder to defeat. It's only a matter of time before her full power returns to her, and you can't face that kind of darkness alone," he said, with unerring certainty. "Not with a thousand oceans of merrows. Not with a hundred flying horses. That sort of magic has only one true match."

Fionn swallowed hard, searching for words and finding none.

His grandfather pushed his spectacles up his nose. His skin was unlined, and his hair was full and dark on his head. The longer Fionn stared at him, the more he saw his father in his features; the more he saw himself. "It's time to figure out your magic, lad. What you did back there to Ivan . . . that *force* that came out of you. You weren't controlling the weather, Fionn. You were creating it."

"But I don't know how I did that," said Fionn. "Or how to do it again."

"I believe there is someone here who can help you with that." Fionn saw the idea spark in his grandfather's eyes—a flicker of light behind the blue. "The time has come to raise your own sorcerer, Fionn."

"But *how*?" said Fionn, in barely more than a whisper.

"Talk to Rose. If there's anyone left on Arranmore who knows the ways of old, it's her. For every dark spell, there is a light one just as strong, lad. If Morrigan can be raised, then so can Dagda. If you both stand together, she won't stand a chance."

The wind blew a sudden gust between them.

The candle was leaving turquoise bracelets around Fionn's wrist.

His grandfather pulled back from him, his face

crumpling. "That's all I can give you, I'm afraid. That's the last of it, lad."

"It's enough," said Fionn, as grief reared its ugly head. "You've done more than enough."

His grandfather smiled. "I'm proud of you, Fionn. Your islander's soul. Your warrior's heart. You're the bravest of us all, lad, you'll see."

Fionn felt like there was a dam inside him, and it was perilously close to breaking.

"You just follow the wind, Grandad," he said, in a watery voice. "It will take you through those trees and down by the strand first. Then just track the headland back to *Tír na nÓg*. Back to Granny."

"I know where to go, lad," said his grandfather gently. "I've always known where to go."

His grandfather squeezed his shoulder.

"I love you, Fionn."

"I love you too, Grandad." Fionn held out the candle. His grandfather accepted it, their hands connecting around the wax as their other ones parted. "Now and forever."

His grandfather smiled, his eyes as blue as the sea on a summer's day, as blue as a sky without clouds. "See you on the other side, lad."

Fionn released the candle, and his hand fell to his side, empty.

His grandfather turned then, whistling to himself as the wind carried him away, to a glowing garden under a shimmering sky—to the woman who had waited in his dreams for ten years.

Another world. Another time.

* * *

The wind brought Fionn home too, the layers flickering seamlessly, as flowers, new and old, dappled the fields around him. The warmth disappeared from the air and a chill settled in its place.

The sky blinked and the lights vanished. The stars were peeled from the sky like stickers, and a silver moon swam overhead. The wind died away, leaving curls in the bottom of Fionn's hair. A robin landed on a nearby fence. It puffed up its red breast and chirped a welcome home, and Fionn sank to his knees and wept.

He wept for the Northern Lights.

He wept for his grandfather.

He wept for the island.

And when all was said and done, and his tears had almost run out, he wept for the darkness yet to come.

Chapter Twenty-Nine

THE MERROW'S PLEDGE

Fionn's feet led him back to the cliff, though he was not consciously aware of the journey. He was lost in the tunnels of his own mind, thinking of his grandfather, whistling in the wind. When he reached the headland, most of the islanders were still there.

Fionn spied his mother and his sister across the grass, with Douglas and Bartley. Tara's shoulders were shaking, her head pressed against Bartley's chest. Fionn watched him plant a kiss on the top of her head and looked away, disgusted. The night was already a black hole of misery—he could not face one more abhorrent thing before dawn.

He pivoted around them, keeping his head down. There would be time enough to see his family. Time enough to tell them of their grandfather's final words, and to grieve for him together. For now, Fionn made his way across the headland, to where Shelby was still perched on the edge of the cliff. Sam was with her, and they sat shoulder to shoulder, facing the dark horizon.

Fionn lowered himself down beside them. "Hey."

"Hi," they chorused.

Shelby took her hand from the Tide Summoner in her lap and placed it on top of Fionn's. "We saw you go off together. He's not coming back, is he?"

Fionn looked out at the glistening ocean. "No. He's not."

"Sorry, Fionn." Sam clapped him on the back. "He was a great grandad."

"He was a great person," said Fionn.

"Yeah," they said together.

They fell into silence, kicking the broken cliff edge with their heels and chipping loose rocks into the sea.

After a while, Shelby turned to Fionn, "Are you ready to talk to Lír?"

"Is she still here?"

"Yes," said Shelby, tapping the shell. "I can feel her."

"Well, as long as she doesn't try to kill us," said Sam, rubbing the chill from his fingers. "I've had enough trauma for one century. I'll be in therapy for years at this rate."

Shelby raised the Tide Summoner to her lips. This

time, instead of blowing, she whispered something inside the shell. Then she slipped off the cliff and onto the rocks. "Come on. Let's get a bit closer."

Fionn and Sam exchanged a glance before slipping off the edge after her. They trod down the crumbling mountain to where the tide lapped up the shore, stopping on a boulder that was sure under their feet.

The water rippled. The crown came first—a sharp halo of coral and bone—and then the eyes, yellow as a blazing sun.

Sam stumbled backward, pressing himself against the cliff.

Shelby laughed. "Scaredy-cat!"

"I didn't think she'd be so quick about it," he said defensively. "And besides, I just saw her eat a Soulstalker's fingers like they were chicken nuggets."

Shelby waved his response away. "Lír, these are my friends."

The merrow folded her arms on the rock, her tail floating behind her in a sheen of silver. She studied them with languid suspicion, her yellowed gaze coming to rest on Fionn. "Storm Keeper," she said, in that familiar oceanic lilt. "At last you found us. With some help."

Fionn stared at the crown bolted into her scalp. Lír, Queen of the merrows. Queen of his short temper.

"I wasn't having much luck on my own," he said sourly. "As you already know."

The merrow smiled, revealing a mouthful of shark teeth.

"I sang you a song," she said, her tongue poking through her teeth. "For the Storm Keeper with the world's fate on his shoulders, I broke an ancient rule."

"I wouldn't worry about it," said Sam, creeping closer. "We've been breaking rules for quite a while now, and as you can see, things couldn't be better."

Shelby snorted. "We're practically a lead destination for Tourism Ireland."

Fionn was still glaring at the merrow. "Did you have to make it so difficult for me?"

The merrow tilted her head. "Perhaps you made it difficult for yourself."

"Fionn," Shelby hissed. "That's a *queen* you're talking to!"

"Should we bow?" asked Sam seriously. "Is that the correct etiquette?"

Fionn shook his head. "I bowed to one monarch today, and nearly lost my soul."

The merrow smiled, but there wasn't an ounce of warmth in it. "We are equal, Storm Keeper. We share the same destiny," she said, rising up from the sea. "One that will lead us into great darkness."

Fionn's resentment was quickly petering into exhaustion. His bones hurt—his heart too. He wanted to go home—to sleep for a while, and forget. Forget, forget, forget. He discarded his bravado.

"Thank you for coming to help us."

Lír turned to Shelby, the shell reflected in her wide eyes. "I follow the Tide Summoner, and she who wields it."

"Good," said Fionn. "There's less chance she'll disappoint you."

Lír pushed back from them, and turned her face to Black Point Rock.

"Can you see her?" he asked, coming closer.

"I can sense her. As you can."

Fionn knew it to be true. If Morrigan had perished, he would have felt it. Her handprint was still cold inside him, his magic half choked beneath it. "She's weak," he said, and the merrow nodded.

"We should seal off the island then," said Shelby. "Make a barrier between the mainland and Arranmore, and keep an eye on the caves, so she can't come up through any tunnels and escape."

Lír dipped her head. "I'll tell my merrows to guard the shores and block passage to the mainland."

She slipped back into the ocean. The waves washed over her, smoothing the surface in a final ripple.

"I don't think Morrigan's planning on leaving," Sam pointed out. "Isn't she supposed to come to power by snacking on our descendants' souls?"

"We just have to get to her before she gets stronger then." Shelby turned to Fionn. "You can use your magic against her. We all saw what it did to Ivan."

Fionn shook his head slowly. "My magic only works sometimes, when I'm scared or angry, and when it does, I can't seem to control it. I'm not like the other Storm Keepers. I'm . . . something else."

"What kind of something else?" said Sam.

"I have no idea," said Fionn. "But I think there's someone we can ask. Someone we need to start looking for."

Sam and Shelby stared at him with blank faces.

"Dagda." Fionn turned his face to the quiet sea as warm fingers walked up his spine. His magic was stirring again—the barest, broken flicker reaching out through his bones, trying to grab on to the name.

Dagda.

His grandfather was right.

Morrigan had risen.

The world was tilting.

The time had come to resurrect their own sorcerer.

Chapter Thirty

FORGET-ME-NOT

When Fionn and his family returned to T*ír na nÓ*g, they sat in the darkness and munched on tasteless sandwiches, staring at the empty mantelpiece.

Fionn knew they were all waiting. Waiting for his grandfather to not return, waiting to know for certain that he had passed over in another layer. Waiting for the pain to come in its entirety. Waiting for it to ease. When they could wait no longer, they took themselves off to bed. Weary feet on creaking boards, long hugs in a quiet hallway. I *love yous* exchanged in cracked voices. Morrigan's return loomed over them, but all their questions seemed to dissolve into grief.

The fight for Arranmore had only just begun. Fionn's

destiny still awaited him; he could feel the murky edges of it, like a ship's sails flapping in a gathering storm. It would have to wait for another day.

When his mother and Tara had gone to bed, their snores rattling through the little hallway in perfect, terrible harmony, Fionn crept out into the back garden. He dragged an old deck chair from the shed and pulled it right under the moon. Then he sat down and turned his face to the sky.

A nightingale settled on the roof and sang him a lullaby. Fionn closed his eyes and felt his sadness grow warm in his chest. The heat trickled into his bloodstream and circled his bones. His tears dissolved in the edges of his mouth and he tasted their salt on his tongue. He tasted sea salt too, and for the second time that day, he felt the nearness of his magic. Grief had pulled it from the depths of his soul. He still didn't understand it, but he tried to accept it for what it was—unfinished, unknowable.

For now.

When he opened his eyes, the sky was bright green. Sweeping strokes of phosphorescence had turned the stars to emeralds. The ring of wax around his wrist was glowing too.

Fionn thought of his grandparents sitting under the same radiant sky, together, in another layer. Perhaps his father was there too. Maybe they were thinking about him just as he was thinking about them. The nightingale was still singing, the garden rustling quietly around him. Fionn settled his gaze on the flowers blooming at his feet. A cluster of purple heads unfurled their petals in greeting.

Forget-me-nots.

Forget me not.

Fionn smiled.

He would never. Not for as long as he lived.

And long after that too.

EPILOGUE

On a frosty Christmas morning, in the waters of a half-forgotten island, smoke was rising above three black rocks. Down by the pier, a band of merrows patrolled the ocean, their yellow eyes glowing in the mist. Snow was falling, but there were no children outside to enjoy it.

By the frosted doorway of the old Cannon library, a boy with swirling hair, and a girl wearing a coatful of candles, stood like sentries. Inside, between the book-lined passageways of Arranmore, three best friends crowded around a dusty map. Sam Patton had brought his great-grandmother's flute, for cheer; Shelby Beasley wore her shell, for strength; and Fionn Boyle had an emerald in his pocket—for luck.

The sky outside was black with ravens. All five of them could sense the darkness hovering on the horizon. But there was possibility there too—a future born of light and hope, and so they reached out for it, with both hands.

Deep in the rumbling earth, an ancient sorcerer opened his eyes.